PUFFIN BOOKS

Pongwiffy and the Holiday of Doom

Kaye Umansky was born in Plymouth, Devon. Her favourite books as a child were the *Just William* books, *Alice in Wonderland*, *The Hobbit* and *The Swish of the Curtain*. She studied at a teacher training college, after which she taught in London primary schools for twelve years, specializing in music and drama. In her spare time she sang and played keyboards with a semi-professional soul band.

She now writes full time – or as full time as she can get in between trips to Sainsbury's and looking after her husband (Mo), daughter (Ella) and cats (Tilly and Charlie).

Other books by Kaye Umansky

PONGWIFFY
PONGWIFFY AND THE GOBLIN'S REVENGE
PONGWIFFY AND THE SPELL OF THE YEAR

THE FWOG PWINCE: THE TWUTH!
WILMA'S WICKED REVENGE

For younger readers

THE ROMANTIC GIANT
THE JEALOUS GIANT
THE DRESSED-UP GIANT

Pongwiffy and the Holiday of Doom

Kaye Umansky

Illustrated by Chris Smedley

PUFFIN BOOKS

For Dashing Dave Barlee and the class of 6B
(Shirley Heath School)

PUFFIN BOOKS

Published by the Penguin Group
Penguin Books Ltd, 80 Strand, London WC2R 0RL, England
Penguin Putnam Inc., 375 Hudson Street, New York, New York 10014, USA
Penguin Books Australia Ltd, 250 Camberwell Road, Camberwell, Victoria 3124, Australia
Penguin Books Canada Ltd, 10 Alcorn Avenue, Toronto, Ontario, Canada M4V 3B2
Penguin Books India (P) Ltd, 11 Community Centre, Panchsheel Park, New Delhi – 110 017, India
Penguin Books (NZ) Ltd, Cnr Rosedale and Airborne Roads, Albany, Auckland, New Zealand
Penguin Books (South Africa) (Pty) Ltd, 24 Sturdee Avenue, Rosebank 2196, South Africa

Penguin Books Ltd, Registered Offices: 80 Strand, London WC2R 0RL, England

www.penguin.com

First published by Viking 1995
Published in Puffin Books 1996
13

Filmset in Bembo

Made and printed in England by Clays Ltd, St Ives plc

British Library Cataloguing in Publication Data
A CIP catalogue record for this book is available from the British Library

ISBN 0-140-37578-3

CONTENTS

The Cast 8

Map 10

Prologue 11

CHAPTER ONE
Cooped Up 14

CHAPTER TWO
The Meeting 22

CHAPTER THREE
Plans 30

CHAPTER FOUR
The Goblins are Entertained 37

CHAPTER FIVE
The Wizards Get a Shock 47

CHAPTER SIX
Scott Sinister – Has-Been 55

CHAPTER SEVEN
Mrs Molotoff Prepares 61

CHAPTER EIGHT
The Coach 64

CHAPTER NINE
A Tent in the Garden 72

GOBLIN NEWS FLASH 1 79

CHAPTER TEN
The Beach 80

CHAPTER ELEVEN
The Pier 87

CHAPTER TWELVE
The Convention 92

GOBLIN NEWS FLASH 2 97

CHAPTER THIRTEEN
A Chance Meeting 98

CHAPTER FOURTEEN
Talk about Red 102

CHAPTER FIFTEEN
Breakfasts 108

GOBLIN NEWS FLASH 3 114

CHAPTER SIXTEEN
Ronald's Paddle 115

CHAPTER SEVENTEEN
Getting Rid of Lulu 119

CHAPTER EIGHTEEN
All at Sea 128

GOBLIN NEWS FLASH 4 137

CHAPTER NINETEEN
Gobboworld! 138

CHAPTER TWENTY
Captured! 145

CHAPTER TWENTY-ONE
Postcards 153

CHAPTER TWENTY-TWO
Scott Gets His Chance 159

CHAPTER TWENTY-THREE
The Mystery Tour 164

CHAPTER TWENTY-FOUR
The Main Attraction 171

CHAPTER TWENTY-FIVE
The Rescue 179

CHAPTER TWENTY-SIX
A Triumphant Return 186

CHAPTER TWENTY-SEVEN
No Feast for the Wicked 196

CHAPTER TWENTY-EIGHT
Loose Ends 200

FINAL GOBLIN NEWS FLASH 207

THE HOLIDAY OF DOOM
Starring
PONGWIFFY
a witch of dirty habits
& sparkling performances from a strong supporting cast
PONGWIFFY (a witch of dirty habits) & HUGO THE HAMSTER
GRANDWITCH SOURMUDDLE & SNOOP THE DEMON
WITCHES AGGLEBAG & BAGAGGLE, & IDENTIKIT & COPICAT
WITCH SHARKADDER & DEAD EYE DUDLEY (EX-PIRATE CAT)
WITCH GAGA & BATS (ASSORTED)
WITCH SCROFULA AND BARRY THE VULTURE
WITCH SLUDGEGOOEY & FILTH THE FIEND
WITCH MACABRE & RORY THE HAGGIS
POEMS
WITCH GREYMATTER & SPEKS THE OWL
WITCH BONIDLE AND SLOTH
WITCH RATSNAPPY & VERNON THE RAT
WITCH BENDYSHANKS AND SLITHERING STEVE THE SNAKE

THE CAST:
THE WIZARDS
RONALD THE MAGNIFICENT
FRANK THE FORETELLER
DAVE THE DRUID
ALF THE INVISIBLE
ARNOLD THE ARSONIST
GERALD THE JUST
TNT
ALSO STARRING:
SCOTT SINISTER
LUSCIOUS LULU LAMARRE
Mrs Molotoff (The Landlady).
SPECIAL GUEST APPEARANCES:
The Paper Thing, GNorman the Gnome, The Yeti Brothers, George the Coach Driver, Xotindis + Xstufitu (the mummies), Ali Pali (Business Manager to the Stars), The Tree Demon Puppeteer, The Arm at the Gate, Squit the Littlest Goblin
Noises Off
Cyril, Call Boy
Music
GNorman, DeadEye Dudley (shanties), Pier Pavillion Orchestra
Make up/Hair
Sharkadder
The Goblins
STINKWART
PLUGUGLY
HOG
SLOPBUCKET
LARDO
EYESORE
SPROGGIT
HRD
PRODUCED BY KAYE UMANSKY
GRAPHICS CHRIS SMEDLEY

GOBBOWORLD
SLUDGEHAVEN
-ON-SEA
WIZARDS'
CLUB
HOUSE
MISTY
MOUNTAINS
CRAG
HILL
SHARKADDER'S
COTTAGE
KING
FUTTOUT'S CASTLE
PONGWIFFY'S
HOVEL
DEMON
BARBER'S
TREE
HOUSE
WITCHWAY
WOOD
WITCHWAY
HALL
LOWER
MISTY MOUNTAINS
SOURMUDDLE'S
COTTAGE
GOBLINS'
HOME
2
1
GOBLIN
TERRITORY
SCOTT
SINISTER'S
HOLIDAY
RETREAT
GINGER
BEARD
GINGERBEARD'S
KITCHENS
(UNDERGROUND
CAVERNS)
N
W
E
S
Scale : 1cm to 1mile
0 1 2 3 4

PROLOGUE

In Witchway Wood, there is no noise. Only the faint hissing of rain falling lightly on to water-logged leaves and sodden branches. No noise at all except . . .

. . . Except the rhythmic sound of bicycle wheels sloshing through mud, accompanied by some enthusiastic bell dinging and a burst of cheerily horrible singing. And through the trees comes a small, furry Thing in a Moonmad T-shirt, sporting a bright yellow baseball cap and with a large bag slung over his shoulder.

It is the Paper Thing.

The Paper Thing really loves his job. He has taken ages to master all the necessary skills and subtle little tricks of the trade, such as the art of Balancing the Bike, the art of Stopping, the art of Steering, the art of Fiddling the Takings and so on – but by golly, it was worth it. Not only do you get paid to zoom around like a maniac all day, YOU GET A FREE YELLOW CAP! The Thing adores his cap. He wears it to bed sometimes.

'I'm seeeengin' in da rain,' bawls the Thing, splattering mud all over a couple of glum rabbits who have unwisely decided to eat out this wet morning. 'I'm seengin' in da raaaain, what a galooooorious feeeelin' – ha! Caught you on da hop dere, carrot crunchers! Yahoo!'

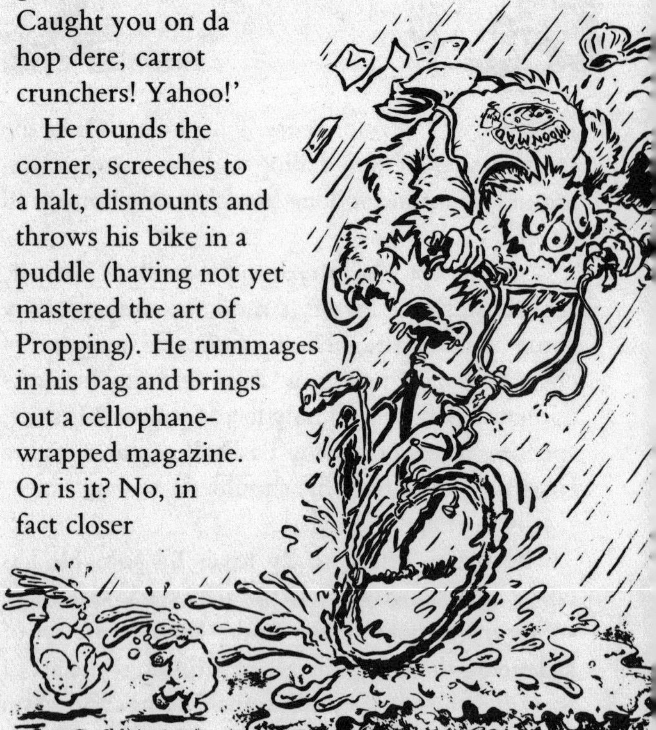

He rounds the corner, screeches to a halt, dismounts and throws his bike in a puddle (having not yet mastered the art of Propping). He rummages in his bag and brings out a cellophane-wrapped magazine. Or is it? No, in fact closer inspection reveals it to be a brightly coloured holiday brochure, of all things! It is addressed to The Occupier, The Hovel, Number One, Dump Edge, Witchway Wood. The Paper Thing stares puzzledly at the front cover on which a group of grinning Banshees in bathing costumes disport themselves in an azure blue sea. Splashed across the top, in a great sunburst, are the words:

The Thing is puzzled because exotic holiday brochures are seldom seen in Witchway Wood. Newspapers, yes. Spell catalogues, yes. Badly wrapped newspaper parcels full of soggy herbs, yes. Final reminders, definitely. But *holiday brochures*?

After a long inspection, the Paper Thing gives a shrug, rummages deep in his bag and brings out a stout wooden clothes peg which he proceeds to clip on to his nose.

He has delivered to this particular Occupier before. He is prepared.

CHAPTER ONE

In Number One, Dump Edge, a heavy silence reigned. It was the sort of silence that descends after Sharp Words have been spoken – which, indeed, they had. Witch Pongwiffy had let the fire go out, and Hugo (her Hamster Familiar) was not amused.

It was very depressing in the hovel. Not only was the fire out, the roof was leaking. Big drips gathered on the blackened rafters and fell with dull thunks into the army of old saucepans and cracked basins littering the floor. Hugo was picking his way between them, armed with twigs and little pieces of screwed-up newspaper. He was wearing his HAMSTERS ARE ANGRY T-shirt, and right now you could believe it.

'Anyway, it wasn't my fault,' muttered Pongwiffy after a bit. She was slumped in her favourite rocking-chair, sulking. 'It's not my job to see to the fire.'

'Oh no?' snapped Hugo. 'Who's job is it, zen?'

'The Broom's. Always has been.'

'Ze Broom is off vork, remember?' Hugo reminded her.

It was true. The Broom was down with a severe cold and had taken to its sick bucket (which was the same as its usual bucket with the addition of a spoonful of Vick dissolved in warm water).

'Well in that case, it's your job,' said Pongwiffy firmly. 'I'm the Witch around here, remember? I do all the important, Magical stuff. You're just my helper. If the Broom's off, the fire's up to you.'

'Oh jah? Along viz ze shoppink and ze cookink and ze cleanink, I suppose? I only got two pairs of paws, you know. Who you sink I am? Super-hamster?'

Pongwiffy considered. It was true. Hugo was a treasure and it was all her fault that the fire had gone out. Now would be a perfect moment to admit it gracefully and apologize. On the other hand . . .

'Ah, go drown in an egg cup, shorty!' she snarled, and the perfect moment was gone.

We have to forgive her. It was the rain, you see. It had been raining incessantly for weeks, driving Pongwiffy slowly but surely round the bend. She was a Witch of Action, who hated being cooped up. The sort of Witch who liked to be out and about, swapping gossip and recipes, popping in on people unexpectedly and inviting herself to tea. That sort of Witch.

It had been ages since anyone had invited her to tea. It seemed that the entire Coven had taken to their beds and were refusing to answer their doors, despite her plaintive cries and loud bangings.

Hugo sat back from arranging his twigs with an exasperated little sigh. Another day of Pongwiffy mooning about the place starting arguments was more than he could bear.

'Vy you not make some Magic?' he suggested. 'Little bit of cackling, hmm? Mix up a brew? All zis rain, plenty of frogs about. Turn some into princes or sumpsink.'

'Don't you think I'd *like* to? There's nothing I'd like better. But we've run out of all the basic ingredients. There isn't a speck of newt vomit left, and all the recipes call for that. I tried to get some from Malpractiss Magic, but as usual he didn't have any. Call yourself a Magic Shop, I said.'

'And vot he say?' asked Hugo, struggling with a box of matches that was bigger than he was.

'He said he didn't call himself a Magic Shop, he called himself an Umbrella Shop. And he took me outside, and there it was. Malpractiss Umbrellas Inc., right across the shop front. Trust him to cash in on the bad weather.'

'Did you buy umbrella?' inquired Hugo.

'Of course I did. It was raining.'

'Zere you are, zen! Take it and go visit a friend!' cried Hugo.

'No one wants me,' explained Pongwiffy with a hurt little sniff. 'Everyone's got colds. No one's answering their doors, even Sharkadder. Yesterday I took her round a lovely Get Well card and Dudley scratched me and wouldn't let me in. Huh. And she calls herself my best friend.'

'Does she?' asked Hugo doubtfully.

'Certainly she does. And she was mine. Until yesterday. Now she's my worst enemy, and I'm never speaking to her again. I'm going to tear up the card I bought her. On second thoughts, I'll cross out the "Well" and write "Knotted" instead. Where's a pencil?'

She sprang from her chair, marched to the kitchen table, pulled out the drawer and upended it on the floor. Hugo shook his head resignedly as she scrabbled about on hands and knees, hurling things over her shoulder and muttering, 'a pencil, a pencil, where's a flipping pencil?'

Then, all of a sudden, she stopped, sat back and rubbed her eyes.

'Oh, Hugo,' she said weakly. 'Just listen to me. I've done nothing but shout at you all morning.

You, my very own little Familiar who's been so good to me. And now I'm about to send my very best friend a Get Knotted card. Whatever is happening to me? I'm changing personality.'

'Is because you cooped up. You bored, zat's all.'

'I am, I am, you're absolutely right. I need a change of scene.'

'Vell, tonight you get ze chance. It ze monthly meetink in Vitchvay Hall, seven-thirty sharp, remember? See all your friends. Have little chat, jah?'

'I don't mean *that* sort of change. Who wants to turn out on a rainy night to go to a boring old Coven meeting? Half of them probably won't turn up anyway, specially as it's Gaga's turn to bring the sandwiches. If I wasn't Treasurer this month, I don't think I'd bother to go. But Sourmuddle says I've got to take along the Coven savings.'

She glanced at her bed, under which the official Coven moneybox (labelled COVEN FUNDS – DO NOT TUCH) was hidden, in case of burglars. And a very good place it was too. Any burglar who would remove something from under Pongwiffy's bed would have to be *really* keen.

'She wants to check and make sure I haven't spent any,' continued Pongwiffy, sounding slightly miffed. 'I don't think she trusts me, can't think why. No, I mean a *real* change. Just go away for a few days, get away from all this rain . . . '

Right on cue, there came an interruption. The letter-box flapped, and something flopped on to the mat. From outside, there came the sound of receding footsteps and the faint strains of 'Singing in the Rain' sung with a clothes peg on the nose, which soon mercifully died away to nothing.

'Oh, goody!' cried Pongwiffy, leaping to her feet. 'The *Daily Miracle*'s arrived. At least I can do the crossword puzzle!'

And she scurried across to pick it up. But it wasn't the paper. Oh dear me no. It was something much more interesting than that. There it lay, all glossy and gleaming, contrasting strangely with the surrounding Wilderness Where No Broom Dare Go (Pongwiffy's floor). A small, square, sunny, bright blue island of paradise amidst a sea of squalor.

'Well now,' said Pongwiffy, a gleam in her eye. 'Here's an interesting thing! Look what's just arrived, Hugo.'

Excitedly, she held it up.

'"*Sludgehaven-on-Sea – where fun, excitement and olde worlde charm combine to create that special holiday magic!*" Oh, Hugo. Doesn't it look lovely? Look at the colour of that sky! Not a cloud to be seen. Just think of it. Kippers for breakfast. Strolls along the prom. Sunshine. Sea breezes. That'd blow the cobwebs away.'

'It take more zan sea breeze to blow *zose* cobvebs avay,' observed Hugo, glancing grimly up at the shadowy ceiling, where dozens of cheeky spiders were currently running around with thimbles, trying to prevent their rafter from flooding. 'It take a typhoon to shift zat lot.'

'I meant the cobwebs in our brains, silly. Oh, imagine going to the seaside, Hugo, you and me. Better still, what if we could all go! The whole Coven. Familiars, Brooms, everybody! Wouldn't it be fun?'

She scuttled across to the kitchen table and settled herself down, thumbing through the glossy pages.

'There's even a pier, Hugo. I've always wanted to visit a pier. There's a Hall of Mirrors and a Haunted House – and it says here "*Star-studded entertainment in the Pier Pavilion*". Oh my! Do you know what I think, Hugo? I think I'm going to suggest it. I shall take this along to the meeting tonight and persuade Sourmuddle that what everyone needs is a holiday.'

'You'll never do it,' said Hugo flatly. ''Olidays cost money. You know Sourmuddle. She don't like to part viz ze money.'

'Ah,' said Pongwiffy. It was a meaningful sort

of ah. 'Ah. But she hasn't *got* the money, has she? I'm Treasurer this month, remember? And what's done can't be undone, *if you know what I mean.*'

Hugo looked up sharply. His eyes widened.

'You vouldn't dare! Not vizout Sourmuddle's permission!'

'Why not? There's loads in the money-box.'

'But zat not ours! It ze official Coven savinks!'

'So? What are we saving it for?'

'A rainy day. So Sourmuddle say.'

'Well, there you are, then!' cried Pongwiffy triumphantly. 'You couldn't get a rainier day than this, could you? No, Hugo, I've made up my mind. I'm going to go right ahead and book it up. I'll spring it on them as a lovely surprise. *Pongwiffy*, they'll say. *Trust you to come up with yet another brilliant idea . . .*'

'Are you sure?' asked Hugo doubtfully.

'No, actually,' admitted Pongwiffy. 'But I'm doing it anyway.'

CHAPTER TWO

THE MEETING

'All right,' called Grandwitch Sourmuddle, mistress of the Witchway Coven, banging her wand sharply on the long trestle table. 'Stop coughing, everyone, I'm about to take the register. The sooner I get it done the sooner I can deliver me summing-up moan and we can all go home. Pass me the register, Snoop.'

The small Demon sitting next to her obediently began to rummage around in a large bin-liner.

'How can we stop coughing?' Witch Scrofula wanted to know. 'You can't stop coughing just like that.'

To prove her point, she coughed all over Witch Ratsnappy, who was sitting next to her. Ratsnappy retaliated by blowing her nose in Scrofula's face, but Scrofula by now had moved on into a fit of sneezing and didn't appear to notice.

'Excuse me, Sourmuddle,' interrupted Witch Greymatter, looking up from the poem she was currently co-writing with Speks (her owl Familiar). It was entitled 'Ode to Rain' and Greymatter was rather hoping to read it out. 'There are only six of us here. You, me, Scrofula, Macabre,

Ratsnappy and Sharkadder. Everyone else is home in bed. It's hardly worth calling the register. It's just a process of simple deduction.'

'Hmm. All right, then. Who's missing?'

'Agglebag and Bagaggle, Bendyshanks, Bonidle, Gaga and Sludgegooey. Oh, and Pongwiffy. They dictated a general sick note which they've all signed, except Pongwiffy. Shall I read it out?'

'Go ahead,' nodded Sourmuddle.

'"*We the undersigned are all very poorly and can't come to the meeting.*"'

'Well, that's a bit of a cheek,' complained Scrofula. 'Barry and I succeeded in struggling along, though I don't know how we managed it, do you, Barry? With our bad backs.'

The bald Vulture hunched mournfully on her chair-back confirmed that no, he didn't know how they had managed it either.

'Bad back? Is that all?' sneered Witch Sharkadder, who was sitting on Scrofula's right. She was dabbing delicately at her long red nose, which had developed a very nasty cold sore. 'You wait till you've got flu, like me. And Duddles has it too, don't you, darling?'

Dead Eye Dudley, the one-eyed tom cat, looked up from her bony lap and leered.

'What aboot me, then?' chimed in Witch Macabre from the depths of a large tartan hanky. 'Ah've got bronchitis, a sore throat, gout an' a frozen shoulder. And ah've got Rory at home wi' foot an' mouth. Plus mah bagpipes have got the mange . . . '

But Macabre was unable to complete her catalogue of disasters. She was drowned out in a chorus of jeers.

'Is that all? That's nothing! I've got all that, and funny little red spots besides!'

'Ah, but I've got all that *and* athlete's foot!'

'I've got a runny eye! Has anyone else here got a runny eye? Tell me that!'

Sourmuddle banged her gavel, and gradually the pathetic outcry died down, finally fizzling out in a sickly chorus of snuffles and sneezes and eyewipings from Ratsnappy, who did indeed have a runny eye.

'Order, order! Well, all right, so none of us is well, we all know that. It's this dratted rain, gets into your bones.'

'Talking about rain,' said Greymatter, 'I've got a poem here which I'd like to read out. It's called "Ode to Rain". "*Rain, rain, you run down the pane. Rain, rain, you go down the drain. Rain, rain, you give me a pain. Rain, rain, you're hurting my brain. Rain, rain, I wish you'd refrain. Rain, rain, you make a worse noise than a train . . .*"'

'I don't think that last bit was very good,' observed Ratsnappy.

Greymatter paused and gave her a steely glare.

'Sorry,' muttered Ratsnappy. 'Do go on.'

'"*Rain, rain, you'll drive me insane. Rain, rain, I wish you were champagne. Or maybe chow mein. And then I'd catch you in a bucket and eat you.*" That's the end. Thank you.'

She sat down to a thin sprinkling of applause.

'Thank you, Greymatter, that was very nice,' said Sourmuddle. 'And now I think we'd better move on to the main business of the evening. We'll keep it short, because I for one am keen on getting home to a nice lemon drink.'

'I don't know why you're complaining, Sourmuddle,' sniffed Sharkadder. 'You tell us all we mustn't use Magic to interfere with the weather, but I notice you've got your own private bubble of dry air around you whenever you go out. I don't think you've got wet once.'

'That's because I'm Grandwitch,' said Sourmuddle. 'And Grandwitches can do what they like. And right now I'd like to have a sharp word with our missing Treasurer. She's supposed to be bringing along the Coven funds for me to count. Anyone seen Pongwiffy recently?'

Everyone looked at Sharkadder, who was Pongwiffy's best friend. Sometimes.

'Don't look at me,' said Sharkadder with a shrug. 'I've been in bed, remember?'

'Anybody else had a sighting?' inquired Sourmuddle.

It transpired that no one had seen Pongwiffy for a day or two. That was funny, because usually everybody saw a great deal too much of her, particularly at meal-times.

'Oh dear,' said Sourmuddle. 'That's worrying. Let's hope our savings are safe. All right, let's move on. Anybody got anything they want to discuss? No new spells? Recipes? Knitting patterns? Cold remedies? Anyone whacked any Goblins into next week? No? Deary me, it *has* been a slow month. What's got into you lot? Call yourself Witches or what?'

'Well, I don't know about anybody else, but Barry and I have been much too ill to think about a thing,' said Scrofula huffily.

'That's right, Sourmuddle,' agreed Macabre. 'None of us has been up to it. There's noo point in going on. We're all run doon. Ye can't make

Magic when ye're run doon. Apart from anything else, your nose keeps drippin' in the brew . . . '

But she didn't get the chance to finish, for the door suddenly blew open, admitting a squally shower of rain, a blast of chill air and a very familiar smell. Several candles flickered out and Sourmuddle's register blew off the table. Barry the Vulture lost his grip on the chair-back and dropped to the floor, banging his head quite badly.

'Sorry I'm late, everyone!' cried a cheery voice. 'Go ahead, start the meeting, Sourmuddle, don't wait for me. Hugo, you can come out now. We're here.'

And in marched Pongwiffy, rain dripping from her rags, trailing muddy footprints behind her. Two pink paws appeared over the edge of her pocket and Hugo's small furry head poked out. He spotted Dudley and immediately stuck his tongue out. Dudley stiffened and dug his claws into Sharkadder's thighs.

'Don't do that, Dudley, darling,' said Sharkadder with a little wince. 'It hurts Mummy.'

'I don't know what you think you're doing, turning up now, Pongwiffy,' Sourmuddle said sharply as Pongwiffy pulled up a chair. 'I particularly asked you to be early so that I could count the Coven funds.'

'Ah,' said Pongwiffy. 'Ah yes. The funds.'
'The funds. I take it you've brought them?'
'Ah,' hedged Pongwiffy. 'Well, actually, Sourmuddle, there is a slight problem with that.'
'What d'you mean, problem? You don't mean to tell me you've forgotten?'
'Not exactly forgotten.'
'*Lost?* You haven't *lost* them, have you?'

'Not exactly. More kind of – spent,' admitted Pongwiffy, adding hastily, 'But don't panic, Sourmuddle, it wasn't on myself. This will benefit everybody. The whole Coven.'

'Spent?' quavered Sourmuddle weakly, hand over her heart. '*Spent?* All our *money*?'

'Yes, actually. But you'll be thrilled when you hear what I spent it on. Look at this! This'll cheer you up no end.'

And with a dramatic flourish, she took the brochure out from beneath her cardigan and slapped it triumphantly on the table, right under Sourmuddle's nose.

'We,' she announced, 'are going on holiday!'

CHAPTER THREE

PLANS

'"*Sludgehaven-on-Sea*,"' read Sourmuddle slowly, peering over her half-glasses at the glossy brochure, on which the Banshee bathers cavorted in the light of a guttering candle. '"*Where fun, excitement and olde worlde charm combine to create that special holiday magic!*" What's this all about, Pongwiffy?'

'That's it,' said Pongwiffy. 'That's where we're going. I've booked us seven carefree, sun-soaked days in glorious Sludgehaven. It's all organized. I've done everything. I've even ordered us a luxury motor coach to take us there. And yes, I used the Coven savings and I know I should have asked you first, Sourmuddle, but I knew you'd all thank me. I mean, look at us. I've never seen such a sickly bunch. If there's one thing we all need, it's a holiday. Don't you agree?' She appealed to the room in general.

The sickly bunch stared back at her. For the moment, even the coughing had been shocked into submission.

'Holiday?' said Greymatter, rolling the word experimentally around her mouth. 'What, us?'

'Us,' said Pongwiffy firmly. 'A lovely holiday in the sun.'

'But we're Witches. We're noo supposed tae like sun. We're supposed tae like blasted heaths and drippy caves,' objected Macabre, who was a strong traditionalist.

'Ah, but you like ice-cream though, don't you?' asked Pongwiffy slyly. Macabre had to agree that yes, she liked ice-cream. Especially porridge-flavoured.

'Well, sea air would certainly be efficacious in removing the possibility of further infection,' said Greymatter, who never used a short, simple word where a long, complicated one would do.

'Absolutely!' cried Pongwiffy, who hadn't understood a word but had a feeling that Greymatter was on her side.

'It says here there are lots of rock pools full of jelly-like things with legs,' observed Ratsnappy, craning over Sourmuddle's shoulder and pointing to the brochure.

'There you are, you see, it's educational as well!' cried Pongwiffy enthusiastically. 'I knew you'd like that, Ratsnappy, with your interest in disgusting life forms. And there's a pier with a Hall of Mirrors and a Haunted House and stuff. And Punch and Judy and clock golf and – oh, all sorts of things. So – er – what d'you say, Sourmuddle?'

All this time, Sourmuddle had been flipping over the pages of the brochure. Now, she looked up.

'I say you're a rotten Treasurer, Pongwiffy,' she said sternly. 'You had no right to use our savings. We're supposed to take a vote before we spend any money and then I overrule everyone and spend it on what I like. It's in the rule book. I've a good mind to expel you from the Coven. For misappropriation of funds.'

There was a concerted gasp. Expulsion from the Coven! That was the worst punishment anyone could think of. Dudley sat up, looking hopeful. If Pongwiffy was expelled, that would mean at long last he would see the back of that cocky Hamster and regain his rightful place as leader of the Familiars. Oh joy! Oh fish heads and crab sticks, could it be?

'On the other hand . . .' Sourmuddle paused – 'on the other hand, I am two hundred years old.

It's time I had a break. We'll take a vote on it. All those in favour of a holiday say "Aye".'

'Aye!' came the thunderous response.

'The ayes have it. Pongwiffy, you're off the hook.'

'One moment,' said Greymatter. 'What about our poor, sick friends?'

'What about 'em?' asked Sourmuddle.

'Well, they haven't voted, and this is supposed to be a democratic Coven.'

'Only when I say so,' said Sourmuddle firmly. 'And I say we're going on holiday.'

A great cheer went up. Disgustedly, Dudley jumped from Sharkadder's lap and went to sulk under the table.

'I dinnae like the sound o' this motor coach business, though,' complained Macabre. 'What's wrong wi' going by Broomstick in a proper manner?'

'It wouldn't be like going on holiday then, would it?' argued Pongwiffy. 'Whoever heard of going on holiday by Broomstick? We'd be a laughing-stock. Anyway, it'll be a bit different, won't it? Going by coach. We can sing community songs and eat sandwiches.'

'Where will we stay?' Ratsnappy wanted to know.

'I've booked us into a charming family-run guest house with lovely sea views. Mrs Molotoff, Ocean View.'

There was a murmur of excitement. Just imagine, staying in a proper guest house!

'One last thing!' called Pongwiffy over the general clamour. 'I think I'd better mention it now. We're not allowed to use Magic. Sludgehaven is strictly a No Magic resort.'

There was a gasp of dismay. What? No *Magic*?

'What, not even *little* spells? In the privacy of our own bedroom?' wailed Ratsnappy.

''Fraid not. The council's very fussy about it, apparently,' explained Pongwiffy. 'It's a law. Look in the brochure, Sourmuddle. It says so on the last page.'

Sourmuddle turned to the last page, and read:

There was a short silence while everyone wrestled with the novel idea of doing without Magic for a whole week. Witches' lives revolve almost entirely around making Magic. On the other hand, if it meant going without a holiday . . .

'I suppose they've got to do that,' said Scrofula doubtfully. 'You've got to have rules. I mean, everyone can't just go around using Magic willy-nilly. Not in a respectable holiday resort. I suppose.'

'Absolutely!' cried Pongwiffy cheerfully. 'It won't hurt us to hang up our wands for a week, will it? It'll be a bit like cowboys hanging up their guns when they ride into town. What do you think, Sourmuddle? You're Grandwitch. It's your decision.'

'I think . . . ' said Sourmuddle, and paused while everyone hung on her words. 'I think if cowboys can do it, so can Witches,' she finished, and a second cheer went up. Everyone leapt to their feet and clustered around her, trying to look over her shoulder at the brochure and talk at the same time.

Everyone, that is, except Sharkadder, who was dabbing at her cold sore, looking hurt.

'I do think you could have told me what you were planning, Pongwiffy,' she said. 'I thought we were best friends.'

'You've been in bed all week, remember?'

Pongwiffy reminded her. 'I came calling, but you wouldn't answer the door. I was bringing you round a Get Well card too.'

'Oh. Really? Well, that was very thoughtful of you. I'm sorry, Pong. I haven't been myself these last few weeks.'

'That's all right, Sharky,' said Pongwiffy nobly. 'None of us has, which is why we all need a holiday. What d'you think of the idea anyway? Isn't it wonderful?'

Sharkadder thought.

'Did you say something about a Hall of Mirrors?' she asked.

'I did,' said Pongwiffy.

'Would those be *full-length* mirrors, do you suppose?'

'Sure to be. You can spend all day looking at yourself if you want.'

'I think it's a wonderful idea,' said Sharkadder.

CHAPTER FOUR

If the weather was bad in Witchway Wood, you should have seen it in Goblin Territory!

Goblin Territory. What a dump. Imagine a stony mountainside with lots of sharp rocks and clumps of stinging nettles and the odd stunted thorn bush. Include a snake or two, some stinging insects, maybe a bad-tempered eagle. And a bog.

Next, imagine a damp, dark cave. At the cave's entrance, stick an abandoned pram, a rusty old shopping trolley and a huge pile of burnt-out pots and pans. Fill the cave with seven unbelievably stupid Goblins called Plugugly, Stinkwart, Hog, Slopbucket, Lardo, Eyesore and Sproggit.

Now add rain. Lots and lots and lots of it.

Plugugly, Stinkwart, Hog, Slopbucket, Lardo, Eyesore and Sproggit, however, were used to rain. It almost always rained in Goblin Territory, so this was nothing new. Right now, actually, things were looking up a little, because for once, they had ENTERTAINMENT. Something to eat would have been better, but ENTERTAINMENT came a good second. (Or was it third? Difficult to say – the Goblins got mixed up after one.)

They had managed to capture a small Gnome called GNorman who, because of the awful weather, had rashly decided to take a short cut back from the paper shop. The short cut consisted of a little path which bordered the southern edge of Goblin Territory. GNorman was aware of this, but had assumed (wrongly) that the Goblins would be safely tucked away in their damp cave, eating nettle soup or whatever it was they did all day.

Instead, they jumped out at him from behind a rock, laughed at his pointy ears, threw around his hat, bent his fishing-rod, put both him and his *Daily Miracle* in a big sack and bore him home in triumph. Once there, they set him on a rock and made him do a song-and-dance act. Some Gnomes wouldn't have minded this, but GNorman was one of those rare things – a tone-deaf Gnome with absolutely no sense of rhythm. His efforts at the traditional Gnome Fishing Song caused no end of hilarity and reduced him to a sulky, scarlet-cheeked figure of fun.

'More! More!' begged the Goblins, clutching on to each other and wiping their eyes. 'Do it again! Please!'

'No,' said GNorman through tight lips. 'I won't.'

'Just de chorus,' pleaded the big dopey one they called Plugugly. 'Go on, go on. Just de bit about bein' king o' de pond. Where you wave your fishing-rod and do dat funny jumpin' thing an' make us laugh.'

GNorman kept his lips firmly buttoned.

'Poke 'im wiv a stick,' suggested young Sproggit. This provoked a chorus of agreement. Goblins know a good suggestion when they hear one.

'Yeah, yeah! Go on, Plugugly, poke 'im wiv a stick!'

'Can't,' said Plugugly. ''Aven't got one. Anyone got a stick?'

No one had a stick. Young Sproggit nearly volunteered to go out and get one, then remembered the rain and kept his mouth shut. The Goblins all looked disappointed. They shuffled their feet and stared at each other.

'What shall we get 'im to do then?' inquired Hog. 'No point in gettin' a Gnome in unless we gets 'im to *do* somethin'.'

'We didn't just get a Gnome in,' pointed out Slopbucket. 'We got a newspaper too.'

The Goblins stared at the crumpled copy of the *Daily Miracle*, lying forgotten in a dark corner.

'Not much we kin do wi' that,' observed Lardo.

'Anyone know 'ow to make a paper aeroplane?' asked Eyesore, not very hopefully.

Nobody did.

'We could tear it up,' suggested young Sproggit, who had a very destructive streak. 'Tear it up before 'is very eyes. Unless 'e sings us that funny song again.'

'I'm not singing again,' GNorman told him firmly. 'Do what you will.'

'Pity we carnt read,' remarked Lardo, eying the newspaper with a slightly wistful air. 'Then we'd know wot wuz goin' on in the world. Fer once.'

Hog nodded.

'There might be somethin' about Goblins in there. And we wouldn't know, 'cos we carnt read.'

'De Gnome can, though, can't 'e?' Plugugly suddenly burst out. 'We could get 'im to read de paper to us. See?'

This suggestion stunned the Goblins by its sheer simplicity. Of course! There was today's paper, and there was a Gnome who could read! All you had to do was put the two together! What a brilliant idea!

'Cor!'

'Fabutastic!'

'Nice one, Plug!'

Plugugly glowed with pride. There was no doubt about it. These days, he was coming up with some real brainwaves!

'What about it, Gnome? Are you gonna read us the paper or what?' demanded Hog, pushing his face unpleasantly close to GNorman.

'Oh – all right,' said GNorman with a little sigh. 'If I must.'

He couldn't sing or dance, but he could read all right. He sat down cross-legged on the rock and held his hand out. 'Give it here then. Everybody sit down quietly. You're supposed to sit quietly when you're being read to.'

Obediently, the Goblins sat. This was novel. This was different. They watched in wonderment as GNorman took out his reading glasses and placed them on his nose. They nudged each other excitedly as he straightened out the *Daily Miracle* and gave it a professional little shake.

'Are you sitting comfortably? Then I'll begin. "*Witches to Go on Holiday! Witchway Wood will be a quiet place next week when the Witchway Coven departs for a holiday in sunny Sludgehaven-on-Sea. The holiday is the brainchild of Witch Pongwiffy. 'The girls were feeling a bit down in the dumps,' she said. 'I thought they needed cheering up.'*"'

'Wot?' interrupted young Sproggit suddenly.

'Beg yer parsnips?' said Eyesore, cleaning out his ear with a dirty fingernail.

'Eh?' said Lardo.

'Did 'e say wot I fort 'e juss said?' inquired Hog.

'Read dat agin,' Plugugly instructed. 'And slower dis time. Last time, you went too fast. You got to wait for our brains to catch up, see.'

GNorman began again, a shade irritably.

'"*Witches to Go on Holiday! Witchway Wood will be a quiet place . . .*"'

This time, there was instant outrage.

''E did, 'e did! 'E did say wot I fort 'e did!'

'Well I never! Them flippin' Witches! They're goin' on 'oliday!'

'I wanna go on 'oliday! 'Ow come them old Witches get to go on 'oliday an' I don't? I ain't never been on 'oliday . . . '

'S'not fair! S'not fair!'

There was a great deal more of this sort of thing, accompanied by much angry teeth-gnashing, eye-rolling, heavy pacing about and the thumping of frustrated fists into palms. At one point, Slopbucket paced heavily on Stinkwart's foot. Seconds later, Stinkwart's frustrated fist somehow missed his palm and connected with Slopbucket's rolling eye. This was the signal for everyone to wade in with fists flailing. For the next few minutes, pandemonium reigned.

GNorman tutted disapprovingly, turned to the back page of the *Miracle*, settled more comfortably on his rock and began to get involved with the crossword puzzle. One Across was tricky. The clue said *Words spoken by backward giant (3,2,2,3).* Hmmm.

Meanwhile, the fight raged about him. If Goblins could write (which they can't) and were asked to compile a list of popular Goblin activities, it would go like this:

Being mind-bogglingly stupid, Goblins really enjoy a good punch-up, particularly when they've got something special to get upset about. Ten minutes later, dizzy and bruised, they all lay groaning on the floor, sucking their skinned knuckles and trying to get their breath back.

'That were a good one, weren't it?' gasped young Sproggit, dabbing at his cut lip.

'One o' the best we've ever 'ad,' agreed Hog, clutching his throbbing ear.

Everyone agreed that it had, indeed, been a fight to remember. Then Plugugly climbed painfully to his feet, lumbered over to where GNorman was still poring over the crossword, sat down expectantly in front of him and said: 'Go on, den.'

'Mmmmmmm?' said GNorman, nibbling his pencil, lost in his little square world.

'Go on wid de paper. But not dat bit about de Witches goin' on 'oliday. We don't like dat bit, do we, boys?'

'No,' agreed the others, clutching at various injured bits of themselves as they came limping back to sit once again in a semicircle at GNorman's pointy-toed feet.

'Well, what, then?' asked GNorman, impatiently riffling through. 'What d'you want to hear? The Skeleton Raffle was cancelled because of the rain. Luscious Lulu Lamarre is starring in a summer show somewhere on the coast. The Yeti Brothers are opening another spaghetti house in Wizard Territory. There's a letter here from some Werewolf complaining about being shortchanged in Malpractiss Magic Inc. . . . '

'No, no!' howled the Goblins. 'We don't wanna hear about that! We wanna hear about Goblins!'

'Goblins, eh? Well, I don't suppose there's anything in the paper about Goblins because, quite frankly, you're not newsworthy,' said GNorman, enjoying getting his own back.

The Goblins' faces fell.

'Nuthin' at all?' asked Eyesore sadly.

'Nope. 'Fraid not,' smirked GNorman, leafing through the pages without really looking.

'Oh well. I suppose we might as well juss tear it up, then,' said young Sproggit, reaching out with a malignant glitter in his eye.

GNorman snatched his paper away in alarm and clutched it protectively to this breast. He didn't want to lose the crossword puzzle. *Words spoken by backward giant (3,2,2,3).* Intriguing.

'Oh, wait a minute,' cried GNorman. 'I've just noticed. Here's something that might interest you, tucked away right at the bottom of page three. It's an advertisement for somewhere called Gobboworld. Something called a Theme Park, whatever that might be. "*A whole world of spectacularly idiotic fun,*" it says here. "*A Goblin's paradise, opening shortly. Attractions will include lots of terrifying and stupidly dangerous rides, regular punch-ups, wet bobble hat competitions, overpriced junk food . . .*"'

He broke off, becoming suddenly aware of a strange silence. He looked up from the paper to find all the Goblins staring at him with their jaws dropping open. They looked as though they were in a trance. It was most unnerving.

'What?' said GNorman uncomfortably. 'What's the matter? Why are you looking like that?'

And in hushed tones, Hog said: 'Gobboworld.'

'Junk food,' breathed Lardo.

'Punch-ups,' drooled Slopbucket.

'Stupidly dangerous rides,' hissed young Sproggit, eyes rolling.

And Eyesore and Stinkwart simply put their arms around each other and burst into silent, heaving sobs.

Plugugly's little red piggy eyes shone. He let out a long, shaky breath and spoke for all of them.

'I wanna go dere,' he said.

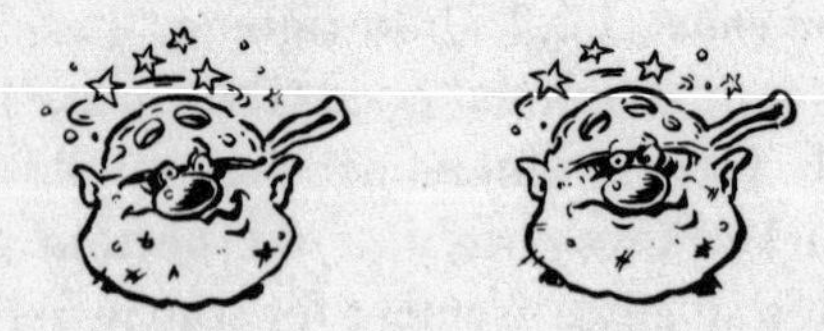

CHAPTER FIVE

'Well, I'll be frazzled with a lightning bolt! If that don't beat all!'

It was Frank the Foreteller who spotted it first. He was sitting in the lounge of the Wizards' Club at the time, idly riffling through a copy of the *Daily Miracle*. One or two of his colleagues looked up from their armchairs with mild interest at his startled cry – but most carried on with what they were doing. Dozing, mainly, after a large cooked breakfast featuring far too many greasy sausages.

'What?' inquired Ronald the Magnificent, turning away from the rain-streaked window, where he had been following the dreary adventures of three little drips with his finger. 'What beats all?'

He could have kicked himself as soon as he said it. If he had just kept his mouth shut and carried on playing with his drips, Frank the Foreteller might not have noticed him. As it was, he came down on Ronald like a wolf on the fold.

'Well, well, well, if it isn't young Ronald. What are you doing standing up, lad? Don't tell me they still haven't got you a chair?'

Ronald flushed and said nothing. That was the

trouble with being the youngest Wizard. You got picked on a lot. And you never got a chair.

Or a locker to put your sandwiches in.

'Dearie dearie me,' said Frank the Foreteller sadly, shaking his head. 'Still no chair. No beard yet either, I notice.'

This caused a ripple of appreciative titters from the assembled company, the majority of whom were not so much bearded as *buried* in beard. There was not a Wizard present who didn't have every square inch of face above the shoulders colonized by some sort of jungly growth. Everyone except Ronald, who had three flimsy little hairs on his chin which simply refused to grow despite being talked to encouragingly every night before he went to bed.

'What beats all, anyway?' asked a short, tubby Wizard by the name of Dave the Druid.

'Eh?' said Frank the Foreteller.

'What beats all? You said something beats all.'

'Oh – right.'

Frank the Foreteller suddenly remembered what he'd been about to talk about, before he got sidetracked with Ronald. He pointed to the paper.

'See the headlines? "*Witches to Go on Holiday!*" Seems the Witchway mob are off on a vacation to Sludgehaven-on-Sea. That's your aunt's Coven, isn't it, young Ronald? Nice Auntie Sharkadder, who makes you your favourite fungus sponge. Hmm?'

Ronald blushed scarlet. It wasn't done in Wizard circles to admit you had a Witch auntie.

'I went to Sludgehaven once,' said a disembodied voice from an empty chair, making everyone jump. Alf the Invisible had forgotten to take his reversing pills again. 'Delightful little place. Quiet. Completely unspoilt. Delicious local delicacy, I remember. Jelly-like things with legs. Used to buy 'em off stalls. And then we'd take a nice little stroll along the prom. Ah me.'

'Imagine it overrun with Witches,' said somebody else with a shudder.

'Yes, it makes you sick, doesn't it?' agreed

Frank the Foreteller. 'That lot running amok in a respectable seaside resort. Witches shouldn't be allowed to go on holiday. They should stay in their revolting caves, where they belong.'

There were a few cries of 'Hear hear!' and 'Back to the cauldron with 'em, I say!' The clock ticked. Then: 'Actually, not all Witches live in caves,' observed a thin, hawk-nosed Wizard, peering over his half-glasses and taking a sip from a small glass containing something green and smoking. His name was Gerald the Just and he had a reputation for being fair-minded. 'And everybody needs an occasional break. Even Witches.'

'Shouldn't be allowed,' insisted Frank the Foreteller. 'They'll lower the tone, you mark my words.'

'Sure to be some truth in that as well,' nodded Gerald the Just fairly.

'Actually, I've heard that Sludgehaven's not the place it once was,' observed a short, pipe-smoking Wizard with a large burn hole in his sleeve. His name was Arnold the Arsonist. His speciality was setting fire to things. 'A lot of riff-raff there these days. And someone told me they're about to open some sort of ghastly Theme Park for Goblins just along the coast. Gobboworld or something. The Sludgehaven Council's been trying to get it stopped, and quite right too.'

Just then, a thin, tremulous sound quavered up from the scrawny throat of the Venerable Harold the Hoodwinker, the oldest Wizard of all. It was quite unusual for the Venerable Harold to wake up between meals, let alone contribute to the conversation, so everybody paid attention.

'Sludgehaven? Isn't that where our Convention is being held this year?' inquired the Venerable Harold in his reedy little voice.

There was a long silence, heavy with anxiety, while the Wizards tried to remember.

'He could be right, you know,' said Dave the Druid at last. 'I'm pretty sure it began with an S. And it's on the coast.'

'Might be Spittlesands,' came the voice of Alf the Invisible, providing a little flicker of hope in the all-pervading gloom. 'Spittlesands is on the coast. Yes, I'm pretty sure it's Spittlesands. Find the letter about it, Dave, it'll be behind the clock. I'd do it myself, but you know . . .'

Dave the Druid hurried over to the mantelpiece and dragged a yellowing pile of old postcards, unpaid bills and ancient circulars from behind the clock. It was a large clock, ornately carved and covered in meaningful astrological symbols. It had a massive key for winding and a big, slow-moving pendulum. It showed the rainfall on Oz, the humidity in Never Land and the current time and temperature in various dungeon dimensions. Its face was a mass of tiny dials and gauges and wee spinning hands. None of the Wizards could work out how to tell the time from it, but it had a solemn sort of tick, which suited the lounge, and was useful for stuffing junk mail behind.

'Now, what have we got here? Spell circulars, "Fly Me" Carpets cards, the sausage bill – ah, here we are. Oh dearie dearie me. Harold's right. What a disaster. It *is* Sludgehaven.'

The small flicker of hope provided by Alf died.

'In fact, I remember now. Brenda booked us the top-floor suite at the Magician's Retreat. That's where the Convention is being held.'

There was an even heavier silence.

'On the other hand,' said Gerald the Just, 'we should look on the bright side. It'd be pretty bad luck if the Witches are there the same time as us. And even if they are, they won't bother us. After all, we spend all our time in the hotel, don't we? Having our Convention.'

Ronald had been listening to all this with interest. He had only been a proper Wizard for a short time, and still had a lot to learn. This was the first time he had heard of any Convention.

'What, you mean we go away?' he asked. 'Have a Convention, you mean? At the seaside? In a proper hotel and everything? And meet other Magicians and Sorcerers and Soothsayers and have intelligent conversations and – and – read out learned papers and stuff? Really?'

'All that, plus a sea view as well,' Gerald the Just told him. 'And you can't say fairer than that,' he added fairly.

'Could *I* read out a paper?' inquired Ronald breathlessly.

'Well, yes. Anyone can.'

'Wow,' said Ronald. He couldn't wait to find a pen and paper and get started. But first he had another burning question to ask.

'Do – er – do we get to paddle?'

He tried to sound casual, but deep down he was very excited. He had never paddled. In fact, if the truth be known, he had never even been to the seaside.

This brought forth a chorus of disapproval.

'Certainly not! The very idea!'

'I didn't get where I am today through paddling!'

'Wizards paddling indeed! Mixing on the beach with the plebs! Where's your sense of dignity, boy?'

'This isn't a holiday, you know!'

'Sorry,' said Ronald, quite humbly for him. 'Do go on. About the Convention.'

But someone heard the distant rattling of cups and saucers, which meant that elevenses were on their way.

And with Wizards, elevenses always come first.

CHAPTER SIX

Scott Sinister Has-Been!

In the curling grey mists of dawn, a forlorn, wind-whipped figure stood by the rail at the end of the Sludgehaven pier, staring out to sea. This was Scott Sinister, once Famous Star of Stage and Screen. His cape flapped wildly about him and his sunglasses were flattened against his pale, thin face, making his eyes water.

Apart from himself and a couple of large Yetis busily setting up a hot-dog stand, the pier was deserted. The Ice-Cream Parlour, the Rifle Range, the Coconut Shy, the Hall of Mirrors, the Haunted House, the Gypsy Palmist's booth and the Souvenir Stall – all lay empty.

Above him, mewling seagulls circled in the grey sky. Below, between the planks, scummy waves sploshed against the barnacled supports. Behind him rose the Pier Pavilion – a crumbling dome of flaky paintwork and cracked plaster cherubs with missing noses. A broad flight of steps led up to the main doors, to the right of which hung a billboard. It said, in whacking great letters:

Not only was he bottom of the bill, they had even spelt his name wrong. Scott couldn't look at it without bursting into tears – which, if the truth be known, was why his eyes were watering, and nothing at all to do with wind or sunglasses.

Poor Scott. The world of show business is fickle and things hadn't been going at all well for him lately. His last film, *Return of the Avenging Killer Poodles IV*, had flopped horribly. The punters had stayed away in droves, and the film had broken all box office records with the lowest ever takings in history (£1.75, and that was from his mum).

Since then, he had been what is commonly referred to in show business circles as 'resting', which in all other circles means out of a job. His pathetic spot in the Summer Spektacular was the first bit of work he had been offered in over six months.

The Yeti Brothers finished setting up their stall and the smell of frying onions drifted towards Scott, making his empty stomach churn. He turned from the rail and walked back along the pier.

The Yetis stared at him as he approached. Their names were Spag Yeti and Comf Yeti, and they had a monopoly of fast food in these parts. Greasy-spoon cafés, pizza parlours, burger bars, they owned them all and ran them all, Spag taking the orders, Comf doing the cooking. They did wedding receptions and barmitzvahs too. They seemed to work in a hundred places simultaneously. Nobody knew how they did it. Maybe they cloned themselves in some mysterious Yeti way. Or maybe they were just very fast runners.

'Yeah?' said Spag, who was cleaning his claws with a fork. His brother sat in the background, sullenly slicing tomatoes.

'A hot dog, if you please, my good man,' said Scott, counting out coins.

'You gotta wait,' said Spag, staring at him. 'Onions ain't-a burnt-a yet.'

Scott tutted irritably. He wasn't used to waiting for food. One click of the fingers, that's all it used to take. But that was when he was rich and famous and able to afford posh meals in fancy restaurants. Now he was poor and desperate, at the mercy of hairy oafs in greasy waistcoats.

'Mama mia! I know you!' cried Spag suddenly. 'You're Scott-a Seenister, the feelm-a star!'

'Well – yes, actually,' Scott admitted, smoothing his hair back.

'Hey, Comf, look-a here!' Spag gave his brother a prod with his fork. 'Ees-a Scott-a Seenister! Hey, Scott! Our mama used to love-a your feelms.'

'Oh, really?' said Scott, reaching into his pocket for pad and paper so that he could graciously give his autograph.

'She theenk-a you're rubbish now,' Spag informed him.

Scott bit his lip, made out he was looking for a hanky and said nothing. This sort of thing was always happening. One slap in the face after another.

'Een-a the show, then?' inquired Spag, jerking his head towards the Pier Pavilion.

'Yes,' agreed Scott. Well, he was. Just.

'Must-a remember not-a to come,' said Spag. Adding, with a leer, 'Mind you, that-a Lulu Lamarre, she's a corker, she ees. Dona you theenk so?'

'No,' said Scott stiffly. 'I don't.'

He clenched his fists and turned away so that Spag couldn't see the black rage welling up inside him. Lulu Lamarre indeed! The very sound of her name was enough.

All right, so once she had been his girlfriend. That was back in the good old days, when she had been a humble starlet and his career was at an all-time high. Then had come the unpleasant incident at a Witch Talent Contest when a certain smelly old Witch – what was her revolting name again? – had taken exception to his beloved, called her a stuck-up hussy and, in a fit of jealous pique, had made her vanish away in a puff of smoke!

Lulu hadn't reappeared for days. When she did, they had had a blazing row, after which she had stormed out, vowing never to return.

He wouldn't have minded – well, not that much – except that she had become a star overnight, calling herself Luscious Lulu Lamarre and taking top billing over him! In the blink of an eye she had become a household name, while he became a nobody. He had never felt so mortified in his life.

'What hotel-a you staying at?' inquired Spag, breaking into his thoughts.

Scott pulled himself together.

'The Ritz, naturally,' he lied with a haughty air. 'Where all the stars stay.'

He wasn't really, of course. He couldn't even afford bed and breakfast, let alone a posh hotel like the Ritz. In fact, it was as much as he could do to scrape together enough money for breakfast. The truth was, he was camping out in his dressing-room in the Pier Pavilion. Well, it wasn't so much a dressing-room. More a broom cupboard really. A broom cupboard-cum-junk room, lit by a single bare bulb, stuffed with buckets and mops and bits of old scenery and smelling of mice. He had complained to the management, of course – but it hadn't got him very far.

Lulu had the big, proper dressing-room – the one with the star on the door and the little lights around the mirror and the huge wardrobe for all her costume changes. And the one and only coffee machine.

'Here's your hot-a dog,' said Spag, handing it over.

Ah! Food at last. Scott's spirits rose a little. Eagerly, he bit into it.

As you might expect, it tasted awful.

CHAPTER SEVEN

'Cyril! Have you got the keys to the larder?'

'No, my love,' came the worried little bleat from the kitchen.

'Well, where are they, then? You know I don't like them lying around, particularly with a party of Witches due to descend on us.'

The door to the dining-room opened and Mrs Molotoff, landlady of Ocean View, strode into the room. She stood, arms akimbo, glaring around. A tiny curved beak of a nose jutted out of her big, cross, red face. She had hard beady eyes and a sour little mouth painted a fearsome shade of vermilion. Her clashing red hair was arranged in a complicated series of nests on top of her head.

Her eagle eye alighted on a huge bunch of keys lying on the table.

'Aha! Here they are. You left them on the table, Cyril! I said, you left them on the table! That was very foolish, Cyril, very foolish indeed.'

She swooped upon the keys, dropped them into her apron pocket and gave it a satisfied little pat.

'Sorry, my love.'

'I should think so. I dread to think what might

happen if that lot get at the larder, simply dread to think. You know what Witches are like. What are you doing *now*, Cyril?'

'Counting the tea-leaves, my love.'

'Well, be quick about it. The beds haven't been made yet. And what about the breakfast menus? Have you done those?'

'Not yet, my love.'

'Well, get a move on. And don't forget what I told you. A boiled egg *or* a piece of toast, not both. We're trying to run a business here. And, Cyril – '

'Yes, my love?'

'Don't use the best sheets. Only one piece of soap in the bathroom. And half a candle each to light them to bed. Half, mind, not three-quarters. And don't forget what I told you. Three to a room, four wherever possible. And no Familiars in the bathroom. If there's one thing I can't abide, it's bats in a bathroom. And if they try to sneak in any Magical equipment, it's to be surrendered to me upon arrival. If you see anything suspicious, you're to tell me. I'm not having any cackling around cauldrons nonsense in *this* house.'

'My love, I don't think Witches will take too kindly . . . '

'Witches? Hah! They don't frighten me. I've seen 'em all, I have. Skeletons, Zombies, Trolls, the lot. Witches are no different. They'll obey the House Rules, same as anyone else!'

Her lips set in a hard little line, Mrs Molotoff straightened the copy of the House Rules, which hung in a prominent position by the mantelpiece, cast a steely eye over the table, moved a fork half an inch to the left and went off to water down the orange juice.

CHAPTER EIGHT

'Well, this is nice, isn't it? Come on, Sharky, admit it's nice. Bowling along in a luxury air-conditioned motor coach on our way to the sea-side. And all thanks to me,' said Pongwiffy, settling back in her seat with a pleased sigh. Up on her hat, Hugo (wearing a tiny pair of shorts and a jaunty straw hat) made himself comfortable and began to draw little Hamster faces on the dirty glass of the window.

'If this dirty old wreck is a luxury air-conditioned motor coach, I'm the sugar plum fairy,' grumbled Sharkadder, in a bad mood be-cause Pongwiffy had pinched the window seat.

'Oh, don't be such an old fusspot. It's a nice little coach. Homely. I think it's quite clever, the way it's all held together with string. I loved it when the exhaust pipe fell off on the driver's foot when he was loading the Brooms into the boot. It's got character, this coach. It could have been a touch bigger, mind. We are a bit squashed.'

It could. They were. Fitting thirteen argumen-tative Witches and their assorted Familiars, Brooms and luggage into one saggy old fit-for-the-scrap-heap coach had been no easy task. However, after a good deal of squabbling everyone had finally managed to find a seat (except Gaga, who had elected to hang from the luggage rack with her Bats). And now the holiday spirit was back with a vengeance as they trundled, creaking and backfiring, along the winding road that led away from dripping Witchway Wood towards the as yet unknown delights of the sunny seaside.

Everyone was really beginning to get the hang of things. There are certain traditional things you *do* on a coach, and the Witches were determined to get their money's worth. There were sweets to be passed and maps to be consulted. There was scenery to be admired. There were sandwiches to be eaten. There were passing wayfarers to make rude faces at. There were songs to be sung.

. . . started up the Witches in the back seat, led by Sourmuddle.

'What a vulgar racket,' tutted Sharkadder, clutching her head. 'You'd think Sourmuddle would tell them, wouldn't you?'

'You would,' agreed Pongwiffy, looking around to see where Sourmuddle was. She located her slap in the middle of the back seat, about to commence a solo. 'On second thoughts, maybe you wouldn't. After all, it is a holiday. We're supposed to be letting our hair down.'

'Mine's down already,' said Sharkadder, taking out a mirror and examining her tortured curls with satisfaction. 'This is my holiday style. It's called Matted Mermaid. I think it rather suits me.'

In honour of the occasion, she had twined a bright green length of material printed with little anchors around her tall hat. Her hair was dyed to match and huge, unnerving octopus earrings dangled from her ears. A kind of Sea Theme, as she explained to anybody who would listen. The Theme apparently extended to Dudley, who was kitted out with a matching scarf which he wore rakishly over one ear.

'Oh, it does. It's lovely. I must say you look very stylish, Sharky. Very holidayish. I really like the Sea Theme.'

'Why, thank you, Pong.' Sharkadder brightened up a bit and fumbled in her handbag for her sea-green lipstick. 'I like to look my best. I don't like to let the Coven down. Not like *some* people.'

She stared pointedly at Pongwiffy's holey cardigan.

'Do you mind? These are my holiday rags,' said Pongwiffy, slightly hurt.

'What d'you mean? They're what you always wear.'

'No they're not.' Pongwiffy pointed proudly at some new red blobs. 'I've painted flowers on, see? Nice flowery print, very suitable for the seaside.'

Sharkadder opened her mouth to speak, then decided not to. Conversations about Pongwiffy's clothing never got anywhere. She knew. She'd tried.

'What's in the chest, then?' Pongwiffy pointed to the huge receptacle blocking Sharkadder's bit of aisle.

'My make-up, if you must know,' Sharkadder said defensively. 'And Dudley's things. His cushion and his catnip mouse. And his fish heads.'

She smiled fondly down at Dead Eye Dudley, who was crouched on her lap, glaring up at Hugo with an expression of feline menace that would curdle cheese. Hugo was retaliating with a Hamster version which would strip paint.

'You should have been like me. Just brought the one bag,' said Pongwiffy, holding up a particularly tatty plastic one from Swallow and Riskitt that looked as though it had been used to strain curry.

'I wouldn't even put Dudley's fish heads in there,' said Sharkadder with scorn. 'Yuck.'

'Why can't you get fish heads in Sludgehaven-on-Sea?' Pongwiffy wanted to know. 'You're daft, you are. I'll bet you can buy any amount of fish heads there.'

'Not the sort he likes,' said Sharkadder firmly.

Just then, the coach went into a deep pothole. Things came clattering down from the luggage racks. Everyone lurched and fell about. Greymatter made a mistake on her crossword puzzle. Macabre's bagpipes went off with a wild cry. Bonidle almost woke up. Sludgegooey dropped a bag of sherbet all over Ratsnappy and Gaga's bats flapped wildly.

'Bother!' said Sharkadder, who now had a trail of sea-green lipstick going up her nose. 'Now see!'

Ribald jeers and the jolly strains of 'For He's a Jolly Bad Driver' rose from the back seat. The driver (a bad-tempered Dwarf called George) tightened his grip on the wheel and did some terrible gear-clashing.

'Told you so!' grumbled Macabre from across the aisle. She was squashed uncomfortably between her bagpipes and Rory, and they really needed two whole seats to themselves. 'Gi' me a Broomstick any day!'

'When do we stop for lunch?' bawled Bendy-shanks. 'Oi! Driver! When do we stop for lunch?'

'There's no stops,' said George firmly.

There was immediate consternation. No stops? All the way from Witchway Wood, over the Misty Mountains to Sludgehaven with *no stops*? After all those cups of bogwater?

'What d'you mean, no stops?' inquired Sour-muddle dangerously.

'Not on my schedule,' George informed her smugly. He wrenched the wheel, purposely swerving in order to drive through a big puddle, thereby spattering with mud a gaggle of rain-soaked Goblins who, for some strange reason, were trudging slowly in single file along the middle of the road.

'I don't do stops on this run.'

'Oh yes you do,' said Sourmuddle briskly, and twiddled her fingers. Much to everyone's delight, George's cap immediately rose from his head and sailed gaily out of the window.

Muttering under his breath, George slammed on the brakes and the coach juddered to a halt. To a chorus of loud jeers he dismounted and stumped back to pick up his cap from where it had landed – the large, muddy puddle he had just driven through. He bent down to retrieve it – then became aware that he was being watched by seven pairs of accusing eyes. They belonged to the rain-soaked Goblins he had just splashed with mud.

(Of course, they weren't just any old Goblins. Oh dear me no. They were Plugugly, Slopbucket, Hog, Eyesore, Stinkwart, Sproggit and Lardo, who were on their way to Gobboland with packs on their backs, sticks in their hands and a dream in their hearts.)

And now they had mud on their faces as well.

'I suppose you enjoyed dat,' said Plugugly. 'Splatterin' us wiv mud like dat. I suppose dat gave you a great big larf.'

'Yep,' said George. 'As a matter o' fact, it did.'

'Let's do 'im over, Plug,' urged young Sproggit, jumping up and down and waving his fists. 'Come on, come on, let's scrag 'im! Let's roll 'im in the mud and throw 'is 'at in a bush!'

'Oh yeah?' said George smugly, jerking a thumb towards the coach, where the Witches had started up a hearty rendition of 'Why are We Waiting?'.

'An' leave that lot without a driver? I don't fink so, some'ow.'

And with a confident air, he clapped his cap on his head and turned his back. The Goblins watched helplessly as he climbed in and the coach pulled away, belching exhaust fumes. The last thing they saw as it hurtled off around the corner was Agglebag and Bagaggle in the back seat, laughing merrily while making identical rude gestures.

''Ow come nuthin' ever goes right for us, Plug?' asked Lardo sadly when they had all finished choking.

'I dunno,' said Plugugly with a sigh. 'But it'll be all right when we get to Gobboworld,' he added more cheerfully. 'Come on, lads. We gotta long way ter go. Best foot backward.'

'There's somethin' wrong wiv that,' pondered Hog with a little frown. 'But I'm blowed if I can fink wot.'

And with great heavings and sighs and doleful head-shakings, the Goblins picked up their sticks and followed in Plugugly's wake.

CHAPTER NINE

A Tent in the Garden

'Cyril! They're here! Have you hidden the silver?'

'Yes, my love.'

'Did you spread the newspaper in the hall? I don't want them treading on my carpets.'

'All done, my love.'

'What are you doing now, Cyril?'

'Halving the candles like you told me, my love.'

Outside, as dusk fell, the parched, hungry, weary travellers clustered at the gate and peered nervously up the path of Ocean View. There was something very forbidding about the scrubbed white doorstep, the thick lace curtains and the various signs reading NO HAWKERS, NO CIRCULARS, NO GOBLINS and POSITIVELY NO MAGIC.

'I don't like the look of it,' whispered Pongwiffy to Sharkadder, who was redoing her lipstick. 'Too clean by half.'

'I don't know why it's called Ocean View, do you?' asked Sharkadder. 'I can't see a glimpse of the ocean from here.'

'You might if you climbed on the chimney,' said Pongwiffy, doubtfully. 'And had a very strong telescope.'

'Quiet over there!' commanded Sourmuddle. 'Gather round, everyone, I'm about to give a pep talk. Now, this is a charming family-run guest house, and we've never stayed in one of those before. The landlady's name is . . . what is it, Snoop?'

'Mrs Molotoff,' Snoop told her.

'That's it. So it's yes, Mrs Molotoff, no, Mrs Molotoff, thank you very much, Mrs Molotoff. Understand? You've got to obey the House Rules. Be polite at all times.'

Sourmuddle was a great one for rules. Even other people's, provided they didn't conflict in any major way with her own.

'Polite?' protested Macabre. 'Ah've never been polite in ma life. Witches dinnae have tae be polite.'

'They do when they're staying in guest houses,' said Sourmuddle firmly. 'I'm not having it said that Witches don't know how things are Done. I want all of you to say 'Please' and 'Thank you' and

'Could I trouble you to pass the spiderspread?' and things like that. Of course, they might not have spiderspread. That's another thing. There might be all sorts of strange food. If in doubt, take your cue from me. I'm not Grandwitch for nothing. I'll show you how it's Done. Right. Put your best faces on, I'm going to ring the bell.'

But she didn't have to, for at that moment the front door opened and Mrs Molotoff, brandishing a large feather duster like a whip, strode out on to the top step and gave them a Look. It was the sort of Look that people wear when they discover something nasty living in their salad. The Witches' best Sunday-go-visiting smiles started up, tried to get going, then dwindled away to nothing. All except Sourmuddle, who glowed away like a beacon in a fog, showing them all how it was Done.

'Are you the Witchway party?' demanded Mrs Molotoff. 'You're late. I hope you're not expecting any supper. Who's in charge here?'

'Me,' beamed Sourmuddle, all sweetness and light. 'Grandwitch Sourmuddle, mistress of the Witchway Coven. *Soooo* pleased to meet you. What a delightful place you have here. So – scrubbed.'

'Hmm. What have you got in the way of Familiars?'

'Three Cats, a bald Vulture, an Owl, a Demon, a Fiend, a Sloth, a Rat, a Haggis, a Snake, some Bats and a Hamster,' obliged Sourmuddle helpfully. 'All completely guest-house-trained, of course.'

'Well, they're banned from the bathroom. And I'll thank you to keep them in order. This is a respectable household and I don't want any carryings-on. That applies to all of you.'

'Carryings-on? What, my girls? Never!' cried Sourmuddle, hand on her heart.

'Hmm. Well, we'll see. In you go, wipe your feet, straight upstairs, four to a room, no bouncing on the furniture, no snakes on the bed, Brooms in the shed, no noise after sundown, breakfast at seven sharp. And may I remind you that a strict No Magic Rule is in force here. Any Magical equipment you may have about your person is to be locked away in my cupboard, to be signed for and returned upon your departure.'

'Lovely, lovely, whatever you say, that'll be just fine,' cooed Sourmuddle. 'No problem at all. I'm sure our valuables will be quite safe in your delightful cupboard. I, of course, will be keeping my wand with me. Official purposes, you understand. You heard our charming hostess, ladies. In you go.'

And everyone picked up their cases and trooped in, meek as lambs, under Mrs Molotoff's steely gaze.

'Not you,' said Mrs Molotoff, barring Pongwiffy's way. 'You with the pet Hamster and the horrible smell. I've just polished.'

Dudley broke into a delighted grin. Up on Pongwiffy's shoulder, Hugo began to bristle as he always did when anyone mentioned the three-letter 'P' word.

'Oh, but she has to come in! She's sharing with me and Dudley,' cried Sharkadder loyally. 'In fact, the whole holiday was her idea. Don't scratch Mummy, Dudley. It's not nice. Pongwiffy's our friend. I refuse to be parted from her.'

'Well, she'll have to sleep in a tent in the garden. I'm not having her indoors.'

Pongwiffy opened her mouth to argue, caught Sourmuddle's warning look and decided against it.

'Will you come with me, Sharky?' she asked.

'Er – no, actually,' said Sharkadder, not so loyally.

'What, you mean you'll desert me in my hour of need?' wailed Pongwiffy.

'Dudley and I are not sleeping in a tent for anyone,' said Sharkadder firmly. 'Not without a proper dressing-table.'

'But you promised you'd share! You promised!'

'Oh, stop all this nonsense, Pongwiffy dear,' smiled Sourmuddle with a threatening glint in her eye. 'In you go, Sharkadder. Thank Mrs Molotoff for the tent, Pongwiffy. Where are your manners?'

'Oh lovely!' said Pongwiffy between clenched teeth. 'Thanks very much. A tent in the garden, you say? What could be nicer?'

'A tent in ze garden, eh? Vat could be nicer?' mocked Hugo as they huddled under canvas later that night. A fine sea mist coiled and curled around the tiny tent erected on the minute patch of lawn which was the garden.

Over in the garden shed the Brooms could be heard rustling around, sweeping their own little bit of floor space and squabbling with a couple of resident deckchairs in Wood (by all accounts a very difficult language to master).

Flickering lights shone from the bedroom windows of Ocean View as the subdued guests tiptoed around with their half-candles, trying to unpack and arguing over the sleeping arrangements in whispers. Every so often, the stern voice of Mrs Molotoff would ring out, reminding them of the Rule about NO NOISE AFTER SUNDOWN.

'Oh, stop complaining,' said Pongwiffy with a

yawn. 'I'd sooner sleep out here anyway. I don't like the look of it in old Molotoff's. Much too strict. And did you see how *clean* it looked? Ugh. And who wants to share a room with rotten old Sharkadder anyway? No, it's nice out here under the stars. Come on, let's get to sleep. We must be up bright and early tomorrow. We've got a busy day before us.'

'Vat ve do first? Go svimmink?' asked Hugo, eyes round with excitement.

'What, in all that water? Not likely. No, tomorrow morning first thing, we're going to hit the pier. That's where all the action is. It says so in the brochure. Now, go to sleep.'

'OK,' said Hugo, curling up with a little sigh. 'But your smell has a lot to answer for.'

'I'm a Witch of Dirty Habits. We must all suffer for what we believe in. Oh my badness! Whatever is that noise?'

From far away, further along the coast, borne on the night breeze, came a hideous sound. It was a combination of nails scraping on blackboards, burglar alarms and dustbin lids blowing down the road. Yes. It was the unmistakable sound of Goblin music.

Gobboworld had opened.

We interrupt this story to bring you news of the Goblins. For the past twenty-four hours, they have walked a long, hard trail beset with difficulty and danger. Sproggit has a thorn in his toe, Stinkwart has a piece of grit in his eye and both Slopbucket and Hog have horrible blisters. Eyesore has come out quite badly in a fight with a baby rabbit and has a scratch on his arm. Lardo has lost his hat. Plugugly's knees have swollen up like balloons.

Sadly, the long, hard trail has turned out to be in a circle, and right now they are back where they started, sleeping in an exhausted heap, worn out by blaming each other as much as anything.

That is the end of the News Flash.

CHAPTER TEN

THE BEACH

'Come to the pier with me, Sharky? Please?' begged Pongwiffy for the thousandth time. She was sitting fully clothed, drumming her feet restlessly on a small rock. Nearby, Hugo waded about in a miniature rock pool, thrashing about with a lollipop stick, hoping for piranhas.

'No,' said Sharkadder, who was sunbathing. She lay on a large purple towel, surrounded by dozens of little bottles containing home-brewed sun preparations. She wore a startling yellow and black striped woolly bathing suit and a large cucumber lay across her forehead (she had read somewhere that cucumber was cooling to the eyes). She looked like a greasy hornet with a touch of vegetable and a lot of stick insect in its ancestry.

'But what about the Hall of Mirrors? You said you wanted to go there,' protested Pongwiffy.

'I'm saving them for later, when I've acquired a glorious tan. Anyway, I'm all comfy. I'd be even comfier if those two hadn't pinched the only available sunbeds.'

She removed her cucumber and glared a short way along the beach to where two Mummies were busily rubbing embalming lotion into their bandages. Their names were Xotindis and Xstufitu. They had been Pharaohs once, in pre-bandaged times, and considered it their divine right to commandeer the sunbeds.

The beach was filling up. A family of Trolls in Hawaiian shirts had collected up a pile of rocks and were marking out their territory. Down by the water's edge, a group of screeching Banshees were chasing each other with a rubber shark. Nearby, a gang of Zombies were shuffling around with a beach ball and over by the breakwater a gang of grinning Skeletons were posing for photos.

'You're going all pink,' Pongwiffy warned her. 'You'll burn.'

'Nonsense. My skin has nothing to fear from the sun's rays. I'm using my own personal range of sun creams,' Sharkadder explained. 'You can borrow some if you like,' she added generously.

'No thanks,' said Pongwiffy hastily. 'My dirt protects me from the sun. Oh, DO come to the pier with me.'

'I said no. Besides, Dudley won't know where I am when he comes back from his inspection of the boat yard. He was a seafaring cat in his youth, bless him. I think he feels the call of the salt, or something. He was singing shanties in his sleep last night. I had a terrible night, what with him and that awful Goblin music. And I'm sharing a room with Sludgegooey. She snores and eats treacle sandwiches in bed.'

There was a short silence.

'What was the breakfast like, by the way? At Ocean View?' Pongwiffy asked casually. She didn't really want to seem interested. She still hadn't forgiven Sharkadder for deserting her in her hour of need.

'Awful. Boiled eggs and weak tea. We all hoped Sourmuddle would say something, but she didn't. Some of us think she's taking this politeness business too far,' said Sharkadder darkly.

'You should have come out to my tent,' said Pongwiffy smugly. 'Hugo and I cooked ourselves a lovely little fishy each over an open fire. Delicious it was.'

Indeed, they had very much enjoyed their breakfast. Particularly Pongwiffy, who hadn't done any of the work.

'I wish I had,' confessed Sharkadder enviously. 'But I wasn't sure I'd be welcome after the tent business. It was a hard decision, believe me, but I keep telling you, there wasn't enough room. Not for all four of us and my make-up.'

There was another short silence.

'I expect you'd like a big ice-cream, then,' Pongwiffy said at last. 'If you haven't had any breakfast. I bet there's ice-cream on the pier.'

'I don't want ice-cream. I'm sunbathing. Go on your own if you want.'

'All right then, I will,' said Pongwiffy crossly. 'Come on, Hugo, hop in my bucket. We're off to find the action!'

And off they set, taking care to kick a lot of pebbles in the laps of Xotindis and Xstufitu, who made a terrible fuss.

Far away in the distance, the twin Witches Agglebag and Bagaggle, armed with jam jars and fishing-nets, were climbing over the slippery rocks and peering into rock pools, looking either for some new pets or, possibly, lunch.

'Yoo-hoo, Pongwiffy!' they cried. 'Come and help us fish!'

'No thanks,' shouted Pongwiffy. 'We're off to the pier!'

Down by the water's edge, Sludgegooey and Bendyshanks had removed their boots and stockings and were having a jolly water fight with buckets.

'Hey there, Pongwiffy!' cried Sludgegooey and Bendyshanks in unison. 'Come and have a paddle with us.'

'Not likely,' called Pongwiffy with a shudder.

'I'm not much of a water Witch really.'

And on she went.

A bit further along, a surly-looking Tree Demon had just finished setting up a rickety Punch and Judy show. Scrofula, Macabre and Ratsnappy had joined an expectant crowd and were seated in the front row.

'Hey! Pongwiffy! Come and join us, the show's just starting!' shouted Scrofula excitedly.

'Well – only for a minute,' said Pongwiffy, who was a sucker for puppet shows.

The tiny curtains jerked open and Mr Punch bobbed up. He was a particularly battered, creased Mr Punch, who looked as though he had been used at some point to clean somebody's bicycle.

'Hello, boys and girls,' he squeaked. 'I'm Mr Punch, I am. Will you be my friend?'

'Not likely,' shouted Ratsnappy rudely. 'Catch me being friends with a moth-eaten old glove puppet!'

'And this is my wife, Judy,' squeaked Mr Punch, ignoring the interruption. 'Say hello to the boys and girls, Judy.'

Up bobbed Judy with a tiny bundle of rags in her stiff arms.

'Hello, everybody!' she squealed. 'I'm Judy and this is my baby. Mr Punch is going to look after it for me while I go fishing. Will you help look after the baby, boys and girls?'

'We certainly will!' cried Ratsnappy, Scrofula

and Macabre, sitting up and looking important. It wasn't often they got asked to look after people's children.

Judy tossed the ragged bundle to Punch, who dropped it. Immediately a high-pitched squalling rent the air.

'Naughty baby,' scolded Punch, picking up the bundle and giving it a rough shake. 'I'm going to have to smack you, I am!'

'Did ye see that? He dropped it!' howled Macabre, unable to believe her eyes. 'You leave that wee babby alone, you tyrant you!'

'Smack smack, smack,' carried on Punch blithely, bashing the small bundle on the edge of the stage. 'That's what I do to naughty babies. Smack, smack, smack. And now I'm going to throw you in the dustbin, that's what I'm going to do. I'm going to thr . . . '

But he didn't get any further. The outraged babysitters leapt to their feet and charged the booth. It collapsed on top of the Tree Demon, who gave a small, surprised yelp. Still wearing his puppets, he crawled out from beneath the wreckage. The watching audience cheered and clapped as Ratsnappy and Scrofula sat on him. Macabre seized Mr Punch, ripped his nose off and held it up in triumph. This was better than a puppet show.

'Come on, Pong!' shouted Scrofula cheerfully. 'Pass over that seaweed and help us slime him!'

'Not just now, thanks. Hugo and I are off to check out the pier,' Pongwiffy told her. Sliming the Tree Demon would indeed be fun, but right now the delights of the pier called and her Magic coin – the one that always came back to her – the one she didn't hand in to Mrs Molotoff – was burning a hole in her pocket.

CHAPTER ELEVEN

To get to the pier, they had to walk along the promenade, which was lined with posh hotels and the better class of guest house. Every so often, benches were placed beneath shady trees for the convenience of visitors who preferred to view the pebbly beach from a safe distance. One such bench contained Witch Greymatter, seated next to a huge pile of dictionaries. Both she and Speks were frowning over an old copy of the *Daily Miracle*. They had been stuck for days on One Across. *Words spoken by backward giant (3,2,2,3).* They didn't even look up as Pongwiffy and Hugo went by.

At the entrance to the pier, they came across Sourmuddle and Snoop, who were busily buying up the best part of the Souvenir stand. Both sported Kiss Me Quick hats and were dripping with keyrings, plastic sharks'-teeth necklaces and small rubber octopuses on elastic.

'Hello there, Pongwiffy!' called Sourmuddle, waving excitedly. 'Come and see what we've bought! This is the life, eh? I'm jolly glad I came up with the idea of a holiday. Are you walking along the pier? We'll join you. You can buy me a hot dog. It's the only thing I haven't tried yet.'

'I shall be delighted, Sourmuddle,' said Pongwiffy. And they linked arms and, with Snoop and Hugo in tow, set out along the decking.

The pier, just as Pongwiffy thought, was indeed where the action was. Merry crowds of holidaymakers thronged along its length, busily stuffing candyfloss and ice-cream and toffee apples and sampling the various attractions.

There was the Haunted House, which Sourmuddle insisted on visiting. That proved a disappointment, mainly because all the Ghosts fled the minute they walked in. Witches are Witches, even on holiday, and Ghosts know when they're beaten.

'I've seen scarier things under my sofa,' observed Pongwiffy, and everyone agreed.

Gypsy GNoreen, Mystic Palmist, was the next attraction. Gypsy GNoreen turned out to be a lipsticky Gnome in big earrings whom Pongwiffy thought she recognized.

'I know you,' said Pongwiffy accusingly. 'You're the same one that turned my shed into a Fortune-Telling Booth that time at Hallowe'en, when the riff-raff came and raided my dump!'

'No I'm not,' lied Gypsy GNoreen, who was. 'That was my identical twin, Gypsy GNorma. I'm Gypsy GNoreen. Either cross my palm with silver or get out of my tent, Pongwiffy.'

'Shall I do it?' said Pongwiffy to Sourmuddle, flexing her fingers dangerously. 'I've got a nasty spell just dying to get out. Just say the word, Sourmuddle, and I'll zap her!'

'Certainly not. No Magic while we're on holiday, remember?' scolded Sourmuddle. Fuming, Pongwiffy had to follow her out. However, in doing so, she managed accidentally-on-purpose to trip over one of the guy ropes, bringing the booth crashing down on top of the unfortunate Mystic Palmist, who said quite a few unmystic things. So that was all right.

On they went to the rifle range, where Sourmuddle won seventeen goldfish, a china wildebeest, a cuddly squid and a scale model of a Transylvanian castle.

'And I didn't even have to fire it!' she boasted, beaming at the white-faced stall-holder. 'All I did was wave the rifle in his face and he gave me all these prizes!'

Next came the Hall of Mirrors.

'Funny,' said Pongwiffy, standing before one that made her look like a sack suspended on scaffolding poles. 'I don't remember looking like this. When did my legs go like this, Hugo?'

But Hugo wasn't listening. He had found a mirror to his liking. It made him look every bit as big and fierce as he felt himself to be on the inside.

'Look, mistress!' he squealed, sticking his chest out, sucking in his stomach and flexing his pea-sized biceps. 'Zis is 'ow a 'Amster look to a snail! Scary, huh?'

'Hmm,' said Pongwiffy, still worried about her legs. 'Actually, I've had enough of mirrors. Come on, Sourmuddle. Let's get that hot dog.'

But Sourmuddle and Snoop were speechless with laughter, falling about and pointing at each other's reflections. Sourmuddle was all chin and knees and Snoop's horns were five times bigger than his body.

'Come on, Hugo,' said Pongwiffy restlessly. 'Let's see what else there is.'

But Hugo was busy posing. They were all having a wonderful time, so Pongwiffy left them to it and wandered back out into the sunshine.

Outside the Pier Pavilion, a crowd had gathered

around the billboard advertising the Summer Spektacular.

'Who's starring?' Pongwiffy asked a large Zombie, who was shuffling away after having stared at the poster for a good half-hour.

'How should I know?' said the Zombie rudely. 'Think I can read or something? Go and see for yerself.'

There was nothing else for it. Pongwiffy took a deep breath, stuck out her bony elbows and began to force her way to the front of the crowd. Summer Spektacular, eh? This sounded interesting.

CHAPTER TWELVE
THE CONVENTION

'Disgusting, I call it,' remarked Frank the Foreteller, his telescope trained on the beach below. 'Shouldn't be allowed. Ought to be a law against it. There ought to be signs. NO WITCHES ON THE BEACH. The place is crawling with them. You should see what they're doing to the Punch and Judy Demon!'

'Let's have a look,' said Arnold the Arsonist, holding out his hand.

The Wizards were stretched out on sunbeds on the balcony of the Magician's Retreat – a lurid pink, turreted, teetering-on-the-edge-of-the-cliff edifice of the type that Wizards go for. They had

taken over the entire top-floor suite, where they proceeded to make themselves as comfortable as they would have been in the Clubhouse back home. In fact, they could almost have *been* in the Clubhouse back home. The only difference was that here they tended to lie on sunbeds on the balcony rather than just sit in overstuffed armchairs indoors.

The Wizards loved the balcony. It was just up their street. Not only did they have a bird's-eye view of the disgraceful goings-on on the beach below, it provided the perfect place to snatch forty winks. Dozing on the balcony came after a disgracefully late, gargantuan breakfast served on silver platters in the grand dining-room on the ground floor.

Also on the ground floor was the Conference Room, where the Convention was taking place – but the Wizards studiously ignored that. After the huge breakfast, they would wipe their beards,

collect their daily papers and troop back to the lift, stonily ignoring the queue of keen, brainy-looking Convention-goers from elsewhere, who took everything seriously. Not so the Wizards. Let others read out learned papers and discuss the relative properties of invisibility and the ins and outs of a pentagram. Their balcony called, and to the balcony they must go.

All except Ronald. Ronald was bitterly disappointed. He had spent long days and nights working on a paper entitled 'Are Pointy Hats a Good Thing?'. He had hoped to read it out. In fact, he had been as good as *promised* he would be able to read it out – but so far, to his great dismay, none of the Wizards had shown any desire to even stick their noses inside the Conference Room, let alone listen to Ronald read his paper.

All they did was lie about on the balcony all day snoozing and looking through telescopes and demanding room service and complaining about their fellow guests (whom they considered themselves a cut above) and the disgraceful behaviour of the merry holidaymakers on the beach below. And then shuffle off to bed at nightfall, when all the fun was beginning. Or, at least, Ronald imagined that there would be some fun beginning somewhere, outside the constraints of the stultifyingly boring Magician's Retreat. At night, when the lights began to twinkle, the faraway pier looked quite festive.

'What's the matter, young Ronald? Haven't you got a sunbed?' asked Frank the Foreteller slyly.

'No,' said Ronald sulkily. 'They keep forgetting to bring another one up.'

That was another thing. He didn't have a sunbed. It was just like in the Clubhouse back home, where nobody had bothered to provide him with a chair.

Or a locker.

'Shouldn't we go down to the Conference Room?' he asked desperately. 'I was rather hoping I might read my paper this morning . . .'

'All in good time, young Ronald, all in good time,' smirked Frank the Foreteller. 'Ah me, the keenness of youth, eh? Ah well, he'll learn, he'll learn.'

'But I thought we were supposed to be here to work. I thought that was the idea of a Convention. That's what you said. You said we would mingle with learned people and have intelligent discussions.'

'Did we?' said Arnold the Arsonist. 'I don't remember saying that. I thought we were here for the food.'

'What about a stroll, then?' persisted Ronald. 'We could at least have a dignified saunter along the pier, couldn't we? Get a bit of exercise?'

'What, with all those Witches crawling around? Talk sense, boy,' scoffed Frank the Foreteller. 'I'll have that telescope back now, Arnold.'

'I rather think I'll ring for room service, you know,' said Dave the Druid lazily. 'I could go another platter of those sausages before lunch. Apart from that, I don't feel up to doing another thing today. Did you hear that hellish Goblin music coming from over the headland last night? Quite ruined my night's sleep.'

With a sigh, Ronald turned and leaned on the balcony railing. The sea looked particularly tempting this morning. Far out on the horizon, a tiny, wild figure with bats flapping around her head went zooming along on the end of a long rope attached to a small red boat which was going much too fast for its own good. (Gaga had discovered the joys of water sports.)

Jolly, distant cries rang up from the beach below where a couple of Witches were paddling at the water's edge. Paddling! Something he'd never done. Sun glinted on the frothy little waves caressing the pebbles. Further along the beach there was some sort of interesting incident going on involving, as far as he could make out, several Witches, some seaweed and a Punch and Judy Demon. And here he was, muffled up in itchy, uncomfortably hot robes, stuck on a stifling balcony without so much as a sunbed.

'Could I borrow your telescope for a moment?' Ronald asked Frank the Foreteller.

'No,' said Frank the Foreteller.

It was all too much.

We interrupt this story again to bring you the latest Goblin news. Against all odds, they have at last reached the lower slopes of the Misty Mountains and have begun to toil up the first slope. So far, they have managed to fall down three ravines. A short while ago, Sproggit slipped between the slats of a rope bridge and fell into the raging torrent below, where he survived by hanging on to the tail of a beaver. Plugugly has stubbed his toe badly on a BEWARE OF AVALANCHES sign. There is a storm threatening, and they have run out of nettle sandwiches. There is now some doubt whether they will ever reach their goal.

That is the end of the News Flash.

CHAPTER THIRTEEN

A Chance Meeting

Scott Sinister (or Spot Snitser as he was now known) had spent a rotten night in the stifling cupboard the theatre management called a dressing-room. Groaning, he unfolded creaking limbs and hauled himself up from the musty pile of old stage curtains which served for a bed.

Blearily, he examined his haggard features in a small, cracked mirror hanging on the wall. He looked terrible. This was no life for a superstar. He felt quite faint. Food, that was what he needed. Glumly he reached into his cloak and carefully counted the few small coins that were all that remained of his vast fortune. Just enough for one more hot dog. After that, there would be no more food until his first pay cheque at the end of the week. If he survived that long.

Not like Lulu, who was rolling in money. Lulu, who right now was most probably tucking into a hugely overpriced breakfast in her suite at the Ritz.

It wasn't fair! It simply wasn't fair! He had more talent in his little toenail than she had in her whole body. If only he had the chance to prove himself, just once more. He'd show them! He could pull himself back up again, he knew he could. If only . . .

But this wasn't getting him anywhere. First things first. If he was going to make it to opening night, he had to keep his strength up.

With a sigh, he opened his battered case and took out a large red false beard. This morning, he was in no fit state to face his public. Better to go unrecognized than to have to run the gauntlet of the sneers and put-downs he had recently had to endure. He pulled the beard elastic over his head and tugged the hood of his cape well down over his head. There. What a master of disguise he was. His best friend wouldn't recognize him now. Not that he had any friends these days.

He cautiously opened the door, peered to left and right, scurried down the dark corridor that led to the stage door – and stepped out, blinking, into bright sunshine.

The pier was crowded. It must be later than he thought. A party of Skeletons in shorts nudged each other and pointed with sticks of bright pink candyfloss as he emerged from the stage door.

'Look at that scruffy old tramp. Whatever is Sludgehaven coming to?' he heard one of them say sniffily as he scurried past.

Out of the corner of his eye, he noticed by the main entrance to the theatre a tall, pointy hat sticking out from the crowd gathered around the poster on which his misspelt name appeared in such disgracefully small letters. Scott kept his head well down and hurried by. Tall pointy hats meant Witches. He didn't like Witches. Witches meant trouble. It had been a Witch who had caused all the troubles between him and Lulu that time. What was her name again? Wiffsmelly? Fugstinky?

He headed straight for the hot-dog stand.

'A hot dog with honions, please,' said Scott, in a high, nasal, disguised voice. He felt quite pleased with himself. This is where the actor in him came out.

'Right away, *meester* Seenister,' said Spag with a leer. 'By the way, I like-a the beard.'

'Just hurry it up, will you?' growled Scott. A queue was forming behind. It made him feel uncomfortable. He couldn't cope with crowds these days. He just wanted to get his breakfast and scuttle off back to the sanctuary of his broom cupboard.

He turned to face the sea with a huge sigh – and at that moment a mischievous little sea breeze swooped down and snatched at his false beard. The sudden air pressure proved too much for the flimsy elastic, and the beard flipped off his face and blew away. It rolled a few feet along the decking, then stopped. In a panic, Scott ran after it.

'Oi!' came Spag's voice behind him. 'You wanna hot dog, you give-a me the dough, huh?'

'Be right with you!' called Scott, making a grab for the beard. His fingers were within inches of it when it took off again, this time rolling towards the railing! Another gust, and it would be over the edge and into the sea below. Scott gave a little sob and threw himself full-length on the decking in a final, desperate attempt at recovery, knowing as he did so that he would be too late . . .

But fate intervened. The escaped beard was brought up short by a pair of disreputable boots. Suddenly, he became aware of a certain smell. A smell he recognized.

'Well, badness me!' said a familiar voice. 'A runaway beard. Whatever next?'

Slowly, Scott looked up and found himself staring into the face of . . .

'P-Pongwiffy?' he said weakly.

'The very same,' twittered Pongwiffy, coming over all fluttery. 'Scott, dearest, we meet again! What a lovely surprise!'

'PONGWIFFY! AAAAAAH!' screamed Scott. And bolted.

CHAPTER FOURTEEN

Talk about Red

'Sharky! Wake up! You'll never believe who I've just seen on the pier! Scott! Scott Sinister!'

'Mmm? Wha?'

With a struggle, Sharkadder awoke from a terrible dream in which she was lying on a bed of coals being blasted by hair-dryer-wielding Goblins in a cave that was heated by a thousand furnaces.

'I said you'll never believe who . . . oh my badness, Sharky. Look at your nose. Talk about red. Good thing I came back when I did.'

'Really?' mumbled Sharkadder. 'Must have dozed off there for a minute or two. Is it really that bad?'

She sat up groggily and crossed her eyes in an effort to inspect the offending appendage – which had, indeed, caught the sun. That's the trouble with long sharp noses like Sharkadder's. They catch things. The sun. Colds. Even flies sometimes.

'It's sort of pulsing,' Pongwiffy told her. 'Redly pulsing. That's the best way I can describe it. I'd say that if Rudolph ever retires, you're in with a fighting chance, wouldn't you, Hugo?'

Sharkadder scrabbled frantically for her mirror.

'I wouldn't look. You won't like it,' Pongwiffy warned her.

Sharkadder found her mirror and anxiously inspected her reflection. She gave a horrified little wail.

'She doesn't like it,' Pongwiffy told Hugo.

'Does it 'urt?' Hugo wanted to know.

Gently, ever so gently, Sharkadder touched the very tip of her nose with a finger. With a howl of agony, she leapt to her feet and fled to the nearest rock pool.

'It hurts,' chorused Pongwiffy and Hugo.

They stood and watched as Sharkadder lowered her unfortunate organ into the water. There was a hiss and a cloud of steam. Small crabs and fish fled in panic as the water began to bubble.

'Ahhh. Thad's bedder,' said Sharkadder, speaking with difficulty because her nose was in the water. 'Whad was id you were sayig, Pogwiffy? Aboud Scod Sidister?'

'He's here! In Sludgehaven! I saw him on the pier! But, oh Sharky, it wasn't *my* Scott. He's but a shadow of his former self. You'd weep to see how he's come down in the world. I knew him right away, of course, being his biggest fan. Even before his beard blew away.'

'Beard? Whad beard? Whad are you talkig aboud?' bubbled Sharkadder.

'He was in disguise, Sharky! He can't bear to face his public. He's too ashamed. That's why he ran away from me, of course.'

'Whad d'you mead, id disguise? Whad's Scod Sidister doig id Sludgehaved id disguise?'

'He's in the Summer Spektacular. I saw the poster. Bottom of the bill, with his precious name spelt wrong. And guess who's starring?'

'Who?' asked Sharkadder, coming up for air.

'That stuck-up starlet Lulu Lamarre, that's who! The one who was hanging around Scott the time he came to judge our talent contest, remember? I got rid of her pretty quick. I said to Scott, "You don't want to go hanging around with her sort," I said. "You can do better for yourself than that."'

'Meaning you, I suppose. I think I'll go back to the guest house, now, Pongwiffy. I'm not feeling too well,' said poor Sharkadder, soaking her towel in the rock pool and draping it over her nose.

'I'll come with you,' said Pongwiffy, putting her arm around her. 'I'll buy you an ice-cream cone on the way. You can stick your nose in it.'

Up on the promenade, a crowd had formed at the foot of the steps leading up to the Ritz. Word had got round that Luscious Lulu Lamarre, dazzling star of stage and screen, was about to emerge for her first photo call of the day, and all her admirers

had turned out in force, armed with cameras and autograph books. Several of the Skeletons were wearing WE LUV LULU T-shirts and a large Troll was sheepishly clutching a bunch of pansies.

'Look,' said Pongwiffy, grabbing Sharkadder's arm and pointing. 'What's happening over there? Somebody important must be staying at the Ritz. Let's go and see who it is.'

'I don't want to. I don't care. My nose hurts. I feel dizzy. I want to lie down in a darkened igloo,' moaned Sharkadder.

Just at that moment, a cheer went up from the assembled crowd, and flashlights exploded as Lulu Lamarre stepped out from the doors and greeted her public with a toss of her curls and a cry of 'Dahlings!'

Hot on her heels came a short, portly Genie wearing a rather odd ensemble of too-small suit, red turban and traditional curly-toed Genie-type slippers. On his left lapel he sported a large badge. It said ALI PALI – BUSINESS MANAGER TO THE STARS. He was puffing on a big cigar and looking extremely pleased with himself.

'Luscious Lulu Lamarre, ladies and gentlemen!' he cried, waving his arm at Lulu, who was fluttering her eyelashes and blowing kisses to her cheering fans. 'Opening tomorrow night in the Summer Spektacular! Get your tickets today!'

'I don't believe it! gasped Pongwiffy. 'It's her! It's that Lulu! Look at her showing off, it's disgraceful. And if that sneaky Ali Pali hasn't gone and made himself her manager! Isn't it possible to go *anywhere* these days without that Genie turning up?'

(It should be mentioned here that Pongwiffy has had dealings with Ali Pali before. Unpleasant dealings, involving treachery and double-crossing and loss of face. Things we don't have time to go into right now. Suffice it to say that, where Ali Pali is concerned, Pongwiffy is not keen.)

'Let's go,' begged Sharkadder miserably. 'Take me home, Pong, please. I've got sunstroke.'

'All right. I can't take any more of this anyway. That ought to be Scott up there, that did. He's the real star. It shouldn't be allowed. Somebody ought to do something about it. And I know just the right person.'

'Do you? Who?' asked Sharkadder.

'Somebody who cares about him. Somebody who still believes in his great talent. Somebody with enough brains to come up with a brilliant plan to save his career and put his name back up in lights, where it belongs.'

'Who?'

'Me,' said Pongwiffy.

'I was horribly afraid you were going to say that,' sighed Sharkadder.

CHAPTER FIFTEEN

Breakfast in Ocean View was a subdued affair. Everyone sat in uncomfortable silence, chipping away at rock-hard boiled eggs under the stony gaze of Mrs Molotoff, who stalked up and down like a prison wardress, pouring cups of weak tea from a large brown teapot.

The only time anyone spoke was when she left the room to shout at Cyril in the kitchen. That was the signal for a bitter chorus of complaints.

'Is this all we get?' hissed Scrofula. 'We should complain, Sourmuddle. We really should.'

'Nonsense,' said Sourmuddle, sipping her tea and smacking her lips with appreciation. 'Lovely cup of tea, that. Eat your egg, Scrofula, and stop your moaning.'

'I think I've broken a tooth,' complained Sludgegooey. 'It was my last one too,' she added sadly.

'Barry doesn't like eggs,' insisted Scrofula. 'It's a very offensive breakfast to birds. Isn't it, Barry?'

'Ah wanted porridge,' grumbled Macabre. 'Ah *need* porridge. She said it wasnae on the menu. Noo on the menu! *Porridge!*'

'Neither's larva,' moaned Snoop. Sourmuddle gave him a sharp glance. 'Sorry, mistress,' he mumbled, 'but you know what I'm like if I don't get my cup of larva in the mornings.'

'Don't tell me about it,' moaned Filth the Fiend, another great larva-drinker. 'Larva gives me rhythm, man.'

'Well, I don't know about anybody else, but I'm starving!' announced Ratsnappy crossly. 'In fact, I'm going to ask for toast. I'm going to say, "Please, Marm, I want some toast." Like that Gulliver Twine.'

'Oliver Twist,' corrected Greymatter, who was well read.

'You wouldn't dare, Ratsnappy!' gasped Bendyshanks, eyes round with excitement. 'You rebel, you.'

'Yes I would,' argued Ratsnappy. 'Can I, Sourmuddle? Can I ask for some more?'

'Certainly not,' said Sourmuddle briskly. 'The menu says egg *or* toast. Not both. It's not Done to ask for toast.'

There was a united sigh. Once Sourmuddle got a bee in her bonnet there was no budging her.

'I wish I was having breakfast with Pongwiffy out in her tent,' mourned Sludgegooey. 'Sharkadder is. They're having sausages. I smelt them. Now, that's what you call a breakfast.'

'And what *do* you call a breakfast, pray?' inquired a steely voice, making everyone jump. Mrs Molotoff stood in the doorway.

'A nice, exceedingly hard boiled egg,' said Sourmuddle firmly. 'Absolutely delicious, and so filling. Isn't it, everyone?'

Glumly, everyone agreed it was delicious.

Out in the tent, Sharkadder paused with a sausage halfway to her lips. Her poor nose was a sorry sight after the excesses of the day before. Even a night spent submerged in a bowl of ice cubes had done little to dim its ruddy glow. Luckily, you don't eat with your nose, and Sharkadder still had her appetite.

'You're joking!' she gasped.

'No I'm not,' said Pongwiffy. 'I told you I'd think of a brilliant plan. We were up all night talking about it and making preparations, weren't we, Hugo?'

'Ve vere,' agreed Hugo with a yawn, adding,

'Vell, you did all ze talkink. I did all ze vork. See my eyes? Zey gone all peenk.'

'They're always pink,' growled Dudley, looking up from a corner where he was worrying a sausage. 'Nasty little pink eyes. All 'Amsters 'ave got 'em.'

'Oh jah?' bristled Hugo. 'Since ven does a vun-eyed fleabag become optical expert, huh?'

'Pet,' retaliated Dudley with venom.

'Who you callink pet?'

'You. Pet, pet, pet.'

'Hear zat, mistress? 'E call me pet!'

'Be quiet, you two,' ordered Pongwiffy. 'This is no time for petty squabbles. Sharky and I are discussing my brilliant plan.'

'You'll never get away with it,' scoffed Sharkadder.

'We, you mean,' said Pongwiffy.

'Oh no,' said Sharkadder. 'Not me. You're not involving me. Not this time.'

'Oh, but Sharky, you've got to help! We're doing this for Scott, remember. I'll buy you a lifetime's supply of make-up! There, I can't say fairer than that.'

'No,' said Sharkadder.

'I'll clean your boots for the rest of the year.'

'No,' said Sharkadder.

'I'll let you have the window seat on the way home.'

'No,' said Sharkadder.

'I'll have that sausage back, then,' said Pongwiffy slyly, holding her hand out.

'Oh – all right,' said Sharkadder sullenly. 'I suppose I'll help. If I must.'

Everyone has their price.

In the Magician's Retreat, the Wizards were also getting stuck into sausages. Great, heaped, greasy platters of them, served by creaking waiters. There was healthy muesli as an alternative, but the Wizards ignored that. Well, Gerald the Just had tried a small bowlful once, just to give it a fair try – but everyone noticed he went back to sausages the next day.

'Anyone seen young Ronald this morning?' asked Frank the Foreteller, chewing away. Teasing Ronald was a popular breakfast sport. It went with the sausages. It got the day off to a good start.

'Can't say I have,' said Dave the Druid, sucking his fingers.

'Probably in his room working on his paper,' suggested Arnold the Arsonist, tapping his pipe out on his napkin, which immediately caught fire. Everyone gave a little chuckle. Ronald's paper was a constant source of amusement.

'Perhaps he's not feeling well,' said the voice of Alf the Invisible. A sausage floated off his plate, hovered a moment, then vanished into thin air. 'Perhaps one of us should go and look.'

'Mmm,' said everyone vaguely. But nobody did.

We interrupt this story again to bring you the latest news on the Goblins. They too are currently eating breakfast. Hog, Eyesore and Stinkwart have lit a small fire and are heating up a lovely bowlful of nice, appetizing moss. Slopbucket and Lardo are arguing over a small spray of berries, which both claim to have seen first. Sproggit has wrested a nut from a passing squirrel and is vainly attempting to crack it by jumping up and down on it while Hog holds it steady. Plugugly has found a toadstool and is nibbling at it delicately, trying to make it last.

But things could be worse. They have successfully weathered the storm and the avalanche. They have made it to the very top of the Misty Mountains. From now on, it's downhill all the way. On the horizon, they can see the clear blue sweep of the sea – and last night, Plugugly swore he could almost see the faraway lights of Gobboworld.

The dream is within their grasp.

That is the end of the News Flash.

CHAPTER SIXTEEN

Ronald's Paddle

Ronald wasn't working on his paper. Neither was he in bed sick. Ronald, in fact, was about to fulfil a lifetime's ambition. He was standing at the water's edge on the deserted beach, about to have his first-ever paddle.

Things had really been getting on his nerves back at the hotel. The constant round of the three Bs (breakfast, balcony and bed) was more than he could take. His treatise on pointy hats still languished in his bedside drawer, unread. He hadn't set foot in the Conference Room because nobody would go with him and he didn't like to go in on his own. As far as Ronald was concerned, the Convention he had been so looking forward to was a complete washout.

All this made him even more determined to paddle. All right, so it wasn't a Wizardly sort of activity – but if he was careful and sneaked out early and did it when nobody else was about, who was going to know? Anyway, he was past caring. He was going to defy everybody and dip his big, pink, flapping feet in the briny if it killed him. Even if it was flying in the face of tradition.

He had arisen at sunrise, sneaked out the back way through the kitchens and hurried down the steep cliff path which led from the Magician's Retreat to the empty beach. Heart pitter-pattering with guilty excitement, he had hidden behind the breakwater and furtively removed his Hat of Knowledge, his Robe of Mystery and his Cloak of Darkness, hiding them carefully under a large stone. This, of course, was against the rules – for, as everyone knows, *A Wizard and His Gear are Never Parted*, on the grounds that once you lose the clobber you lose the dignity.

Some while later he had emerged self-consciously clad in a pair of large, bright yellow shorts which he had secretly purchased from a souvenir shop the day before (under the pretext of popping out for a pencil sharpener). He had loved the look of them in the window, but now he had them on, he wasn't so sure. He had a niggling feeling they didn't do a lot for his knees. Draped around his neck was a towel emblazoned with the words HOTEL PROPERTY – DO NOT REMOVE. He felt horribly naked.

The sea was a long way out, and it had taken him a long time to pick his way over the millions of excruciatingly sharp pebbles and acres of smelly, slippery seaweed that lay between him and the water's edge. There was a chilly wind too, which blew up his shorts most unpleasantly.

But at last, he made it. Arms clutched across his skinny chest, he balanced stork-like on one thin white leg and dipped an experimental toe in the water.

Brrr. It was freezing. Still, he had set out to paddle – and paddle he jolly well would. At least he'd have one happy memory to take home with him at the end of it all.

Shivering, he took a deep breath and waded out into the cold grey water.

Far behind him, on the beach, unobserved by Ronald, two small Troll children overturned the stone and made off with his clothes, just for a laugh.

And that was only the first bad thing that happened.

CHAPTER SEVENTEEN

Getting Rid of Lulu

Lulu Lamarre was seated before her dressing-table mirror, trying to decide which wig to wear. She had risen late, after a luxurious breakfast in bed. That's one of the advantages of being a superstar and staying in the top hotels. You can have breakfast in bed any time you like. You can order what you like too and nobody will bat an eyelid. Lulu had chosen chips, tuna fish, chocolate cake and a cherry float with a side order of ketchup. And very nice it had been too.

Now then. Which wig? After a bit of thought, Lulu decided on the long blonde curly one. She pulled it on, fluffed it up, batted her eyelashes and smiled complacently at her reflection.

Lulu had been doing a lot of complacent smiling recently. She had come a long way since the early days when she was a mere extra, hanging around the edges of show business. Her career was really beginning to take off. Lulu Lamarre was fast becoming a household name. Just one more well-paid film, that's all it would take, and she would be able to buy herself that rather nice holiday retreat on the other side of Witchway Wood. The one that used to be owned by Scott Sinister, her ex-boyfriend.

Hah! That'd show him.

There came a discreet tap at the bedroom door.

'Come in,' purred Lulu huskily, fluffing up her frilly robe and adopting a glamorous pose.

The door opened, and in came a creaking old waiter with a paper bag over his head(?) bearing a grubby envelope on a silver tray.

'A letter for you, Miss Lamarre. Handed in at reception early this morning.'

'For me? Oh, how adorable!' cried Lulu, snatching it up. 'I wonder who can be writing to me? One of my many fans, I suppose. All right, servant, you can clear off now.'

Eagerly she tore it open, and read:

Dear Miss Lamarre

It has cum to my attenshun that you are starring in the Summer Spektacular at the Pavilliun. I am a Millyonair film prodooser and rite now I am hollydaying On my fabulus luckshoory ~~Yacght~~ ~~Yoght~~ Yot in the next bay. I wood very much lik you to star in my neckst blokbuster. I will pay you a lot. You will be sucksessfull beyond yore wildest dreems. Plees cum to the old jetty in the bote yard at ten O'clock sharp. You will be piked up by my trusty old boteman who will row you out to my ~~Youcht~~ ~~Ychat~~ Yot and we can diskus a skreen test over a glass of ~~champayn~~ ~~Shampagn~~. ~~sheampam~~ wine. Yores sinseeerly

~~[illegible]~~ (millyonair)

Sebastien B. Jetsetter (millyonair)

P.S cum alone. Dote tel anywun

She should have been suspicious, of course. The spellings alone should have told her something, as should the crossings-out, fingermarks and general disgustingly grubby state of the thing. But being a superstar doesn't necessarily mean you have to be intelligent.

With a little squeal of excitement, Lulu leapt to her feet and launched herself at her wardrobe.

'This isn't going to work, I tell you!' said Sharkadder nervously. She was standing on the jetty with Pongwiffy and Dudley, casting dark glances at the small rowing-boat bobbing about at the foot of a flight of slippery steps.

She was wearing a long black oilskin, matching sou'wester and a pair of thick-soled rubber boots, all of which had been hired by Pongwiffy at great personal expense. (Well, it would have been, if she hadn't used her magic coin.) Dudley was crouched on the top of a nearby lobster pot, chewing on a fish head and growling every time anyone came near.

'Of course it'll work. You make a very convincing boatman. Your nose in particular has got a real weatherbeaten look about it.'

'Why can't you be the boatman?' cried Sharkadder, stamping her rubber-booted foot. 'I don't know anything about boats! Why does it have to be me?'

'Because she knows me and she doesn't know you, that's why. Look, it'll be fine. Just talk about port and starboard and say Arrr and Avast and Belay and things like that. Spit in the wind. Get Dudley to sing one of his sea shanties. On second thoughts, I should only use that in an emergency.'

'Which is port?' asked Sharkadder, all flustered.

'I don't know. The sharp end. Who cares?' said Pongwiffy vaguely. 'She won't know the difference anyway. The most important thing is to get her into the boat and away from the harbour. Once we're into the open sea, we can all relax. Me and Hugo will come out from hiding under the tarpaulin and take over the oars.'

'Which are the oars?' inquired Sharkadder.

'They're the long stick-type things you put in the water,' explained Pongwiffy a touch impatiently. 'There's nothing to it. Just dip 'em in and splash 'em about a bit, and the boat'll move.'

'Yes, but which way?' said Sharkadder worriedly.

'Forwards, hopefully.'

'As long as it's not down,' said Sharkadder doubtfully. 'Look, Pong, I really don't think this is a good idea.'

'Yes it is. It's brilliant. We simply row out to sea and maroon her on a rock for a few days. Just to keep her out of the way long enough for Scott to have his chance. He'll take over the show at a minute's notice and get rave reviews. It's bound to work. It always does in books.'

'We're not in a book,' said Sharkadder. 'This is

real. That's real wet water down there and I'm not at all sure that boat's seaworthy.'

'Of course it's seaworthy. Trust you to pick holes in my plan.'

'It's holes in the boat I'm worried about,' fretted Sharkadder.

'Nonsense. It'll work like a dream. We'll go back and pick Lulu up later, when Scott's a star again and everyone's forgotten about her. You know how it is in the world of show business. Out of sight, out of mind. Here today, gone tomorrow. Easy come, easy g . . . '

'Mistress!' Hugo emerged from a dark alley where he had been posted as lookout and came running towards them across the cobbles, eyes bulging. 'It her! She comink!'

'Right, this is it. Come on, Hugo, down into the boat. It's all up to you now, Sharky. Don't let me down.'

The two of them hurried down the steps and climbed into the rocking boat. They lay down and pulled the tarpaulin over them just as Lulu emerged from the alley and stood looking about her hesitantly. She was wearing her most diaphanous gown, her most glittery jewellery and highly unsuitable high-heeled gold sandals. This was her big chance and she was obviously intent on making an impression.

Sharkadder cleared her throat nervously. 'Step this way, lady,' she called. 'All aboard for Mr Jetsetter's luxury yacht. Arrr.'

'Are you the boatman?' demanded Lulu imperiously, teetering unsteadily along the jetty.

'Avast and belay, I certainly am,' agreed Sharkadder. 'That's me. Just a salty old seadog who knows all about port and starboard and things. And this is my trusty ship's cat. Excuse me while I spit in the wind. Step right down into the boat, and sit down the blunt end, well away from the tarpaulin. There's a whole pile of dead fish under there and I don't want 'em disturbed. Arrr.'

Lulu gathered up her gown, gingerly picked her way down the slippery steps and clambered into the boat, which wobbled alarmingly.

'I see what you mean about the fish,' she said, wrinkling her nose and staring about her disdainfully. 'It's very smelly in this boat. And why isn't there a cushion? I must say I'm very surprised a millionaire like Mr Jetsetter can't afford something a bit better for his guests.'

'Nothing wrong with my boat,' protested Sharkadder with a heartiness she didn't feel. She climbed in and groped her way unsteadily to the helm. 'All right, Dudley, you can cast off now. No, there's nothing wrong with the good old Saucy Sal. Arrr.'

'Saucy Sal? I thought it said Bouncing Billy on the side,' said Lulu suspiciously.

'Oh, does it?' said Sharkadder, affecting vague surprise. 'I wonder who changed that, then. Hurry up, Dudley, leave that fish head and untie the rope. We have to catch the tide, remember?'

The rope tethering the boat slithered down with a thump, closely followed by Dudley. Sharkadder picked up an oar and pushed with all her might against the jetty. Rocking wildly, the boat shot out across the water, surprising everyone. Sharkadder wobbled and flailed her arms wildly, letting go of the oar, which fell over the side with a splash and floated away in the opposite direction. With a little shriek, Sharkadder fell over backwards to the bottom of the boat, where she lay with her legs kicking feebly in the air in a most unboatmanlike manner. Lulu gave a sharp scream and clutched at the sides.

'What's happening?' she squealed as the boat got caught in an eddy and began to spin in circles.

'Don't panic!' cried Sharkadder, picking herself up and grabbing for the one remaining oar. 'Everything's under control. I'll just steady us up a bit. Arrr.'

'Let me off this minute!' demanded Lulu. 'I don't believe you're Mr Jetsetter's boatman at all. In fact, I don't believe there *is* a Mr Jetsetter! I think this is all a trick!'

And she attempted to stand up. At the same time, Sharkadder made a great, despairing dig at the water. The boat spun wildly. Sharkadder lost her balance for the second time, this time falling forward on to the heaped tarpaulin in the bottom of the boat. There was a muffled cry of pain and the tarpaulin gave a convulsive heave.

'Ahhhha!' screamed Lulu, pointing with a trembling finger. 'The fish! The fish! They're coming alive! They're . . . '

'Oh, stop your blithering!' said an irritable voice. 'Honestly, Sharky, can't you do *anything*? Give me that oar and get out of the way before you have us over.'

And to Lulu's horror, she found herself staring into the dreaded countenance of her old enemy.

CHAPTER EIGHTEEN

'I thought you said you could row,' taunted Sharkadder as the current swirled the boat out to sea. "Nothing to it," you said. "I'll come out of hiding and take over the oars," you said. I distinctly heard you say it.'

'Help!' screeched Lulu in her ear. 'Help! Help me, someone!'

'Well, I can hardly row with only one oar, can I?' objected Pongwiffy. 'And we all know whose fault *that* is.'

'Help!' bawled Lulu. 'Call the coastguards! Boxing Day! Boxing Day!'

'I think it's May Day, actually,' Pongwiffy told her. 'And shut up,' she added as an afterthought.

'I said all along I didn't want to be boatman,' said Sharkadder crossly. 'Don't blame me. It's all your fault that we're lost at sea. This is the last time I go along with any of your half-baked ideas.'

'Half-baked idea? You're talking about an ingenious plan, worked out to the last detail. Or it was, until you mucked it up. Anyway, we're not lost at sea. We're merely temporarily caught in a fast-moving current.'

'Which is hurtling us to our doom,' said Sharkadder darkly.

'HELP! HELP! HEEEEELP!'

'Of course it's not,' scoffed Pongwiffy. 'Now see what you've done. You've set her off again with all your talk of doom.'

'I don't care, it's true. In fact, this whole holiday was doomed from the outset. That's because it was your idea.'

'Oh, don't be such an old grouch! Anyway, we're only just out of the harbour. You can see the beach from here. Besides, Hugo knows what to do, don't you, Hugo? He's been shipwrecked off Cape Horn, he told me. Haven't you Hugo?'

But Hugo had gone pale green and didn't answer.

'Not much help there,' said Sharkadder cuttingly, adding, 'But then, what do you expect from a Hamster? It's lucky we have my Dudley. He can share his seafaring knowledge with us. What do we do next, Duddles, darling? Tell Mummy.'

But Dudley had his head over the side and was groaning loudly.

'Well, that's just terrific,' said Pongwiffy, disgusted. 'Perhaps we are hurtling to our doom after all.'

'HEEEEEEELLLLP! HELLLLPPPP!'

'I thought I told you to shut up,' she told Lulu.

'Why should I? You're just a couple of spiteful old Witches out to get me. You've always had it in for me. What have I ever done to you?'

'You've ruined Scott's career, that's what,'

snapped Pongwiffy. 'You've taken his rightful place at The Top. But you reckoned without us. We're going to dump you on a deserted rock for a day or two. That'll teach you to steal his thunder.'

'You can't do that! What about my public? It's opening night and I'm the star!'

'Not any more you're not. Scott's going to Save The Show and after that you'll be lucky if you get a walk-on part. So there.'

'I hate to be a spoilsport, Pong, but I don't actually see any deserted rocks,' pointed out Sharkadder. 'And even if I did, we'd probably swish right past. We seem to be rather at the mercy of the current, don't you know.'

'Well, that's just where you're wrong, because look what's ahead!' Pongwiffy pointed triumphantly. 'If that's not a rock, what is it? That tall, thin, greyish thing sticking up out of the water.'

'It's a person,' said Sharkadder, squinting. 'A person stranded on a sandbank, by the look of it. In fact, unless I'm very much mistaken, I do believe it's my nephew Ronald.'

'Oh botheration,' said Pongwiffy, who didn't like Sharkadder's nephew Ronald. 'That's all we need.'

'Ssh. I think he's shouting something. It sounds like . . .'

'HEEEEELLLLPPPP!' screeched Lulu, getting a second wind.

'That's it,' agreed Sharkadder. 'Cooeee! Ronald! What are you doing on that sandbank? And wearing those hideous yellow shorts? Have you no fashion sense?'

'I'm stranded!' came the faint cry. 'Help me, Aunt Sharkadder!'

'Shall we? What do you think?' Sharkadder asked Pongwiffy.

'No,' said Pongwiffy firmly. 'Anyone who wears shorts like that doesn't deserve to be rescued.'

'Mmm. You have a point. Oh well, I suppose I'd better. After all, he is Family. All right, Ronald, we're coming. Be ready to grab the oar as we go past! Hold out the oar, Pongwiffy, we're going to rescue Ronald.'

'Why?' asked Pongwiffy, stubbornly clutching the oar to herself. 'He calls himself a Wizard, doesn't he? Why can't he rescue himself?'

'Oh, give it me, I'll do it! Come on, before it's too late.'

She held out her hand. Reluctantly Pongwiffy surrendered the oar and Sharkadder stuck it out over the side of the boat at arm's length as the boat came level with Ronald. He reached out desperately clutching fingers and caught it. The boat slowed just long enough for Sharkadder to grab a handful of shorts and haul him in over the side. He toppled in and fell to the bottom, white, wheezing, whimpering and extremely wet.

'Ugh!' said Lulu, hastily drawing her feet away. 'He's all soggy. What have we got to have *him* for?'

'My sentiments entirely,' Pongwiffy agreed. 'That's the first sensible thing I've ever heard you say. You're just an old softy, Sharkadder. It's too crowded in this boat. Look how we're shipping water.'

'Sit up, Ronald,' Sharkadder instructed severely. 'I have a few questions to ask you, and I want some straight answers. I asked you what you think you're doing, stranded on a sandbank in the middle of the ocean.'

Ronald rolled over, sat up and mumbled something.

'What? Speak up, I didn't quite hear.'

'I said I was paddling,' muttered Ronald, wringing out his shorts.

'Paddling? Not a very Wizardly occupation, is it? What are you doing in Sludgehaven anyway? And where are your lovely robes? And most important, who told you you could wear shorts with *those* knees?'

But Ronald wasn't listening. He had just noticed Lulu. His jaw went slack and a silly look came over his face.

'I say,' he said. 'I say, aren't you Luscious Lulu Lamarre, the superstar?'

'Well, yes,' admitted Lulu, tossing her hair and preening a bit despite her desperate situation. 'I am, actually.'

'Gosh,' said Ronald, quite overcome. 'Gosh. I'm a big fan of yours. Can I have your autograph?'

'Well, yes of course, I . . . '

'No you can't,' broke in Pongwiffy crossly. 'Let's throw him overboard, Sharkadder, he's getting on my nerves.'

'He's my nephew, Pongwiffy. If there's any throwing overboard to be done, I'll decide. I asked you what you're doing in Sludgehaven, Ronald. Apart from drowning.'

'Having a Convention,' mumbled Ronald sheepishly, shivering and crossing his arms over his puny chest. 'We're all staying up at the Magician's Retreat. It's a very serious sort of thing. I – er – just slipped out for a quick paddle and the tide sort of came in when I wasn't looking. You – er – you won't tell the others, will you, Auntie?'

'*I* will,' promised Pongwiffy with relish. 'I'm going to tell everybody, the minute we land.'

'If we ever do land,' remarked Sharkadder, and Lulu burst into loud sobs.

Indeed, the possibility of landing was becoming ever more remote. The current was fairly zipping along, and the beach was now out of sight. They had rounded the headland, and the coastline was an unfamiliar vista of craggy, towering cliffs and sharp rocks, wet with crashing surf.

'Listen,' said Sharkadder, cupping her ear. 'I think I can hear something.'

She could. Across the waves came a ghastly drone, interspersed with various tinklings and crashings.

'Goblin music,' said Pongwiffy grimly. 'We must be getting near to Gobboworld. What a racket. I can't stand this. There's nothing else for it. We'll have to use Magic.'

'We're not allowed,' Sharkadder reminded her. 'No Magic in Sludgehaven, remember? Anyway, we haven't got our wands.'

'Ah, but we're not exactly *in* Sludgehaven, are we? We're at sea. That's different,' argued Pongwiffy. 'And I don't need a wand,' she added. 'I'll just do a tiny little landing spell, off the top of my head, and get the boat to take us to a suitable rock. Then we can drop off Lulu and get back in time to see Scott's moment of glorious triumph.'

'Oh no!' cried Sharkadder. 'You're not using one of those wonky old spells of yours. Don't! You know they never wor . . . '

But she was too late. Pongwiffy had already started. She flexed her fingers and screwed her eyes tight shut, concentrating.

'Wind and waves, now hear my cry!
Take us to a rock nearby,
O'er the sea now let us float
In this little rowing-boat.'

'There. That should do it. What's happening?'

'We're sinking,' Sharkadder told her sadly.

And indeed, they were.

Time now for the latest update on the Goblins. We join them as they are standing up on the cliff, staring out to sea. They have just seen something of interest. Something that has caused their faces to brighten and the blood to pound in their veins.

They need cheering up, because something terrible has just happened. Their hopes have all been dashed. Their worst nightmare has just come true.

They have been refused entry to Gobboworld!

The way it happened was . . .

No. Enough of these snippets. After all they've been through, the very least they deserve is a chapter all to themselves.

CHAPTER NINETEEN

'GOBBOWORLD! We made it!' gasped Lardo. And he burst into tears.

The Goblins stood in a swaying huddle, staring up in awe at the towering gates with their huge, neon-lit sign. In true Goblin fashion, neither of the Bs that spelt out the name were working, turning the name into Gooworld – but Goblins can't read, so it hardly mattered. From within came the sound of wildly pumping music, wailing sirens and thin, high-pitched screaming.

'Well,' said Plugugly. 'Dis is it, boys. End o' de line. De answer to all our wassits. Dem pichers you get when you sleeps.'

'Dreams,' said Slopbucket, excelling himself.

'Mine 'ave usually got alligators in,' remarked Eyesore vaguely.

'So what are we waiting for?' squawked Sproggit, jumping up and down, beside himself with excitement. 'Come on, come on, less go!'

Hearts hammering with anticipation, they once again picked up their sore feet and limped to the turnstile, which barred their entrance.

There was a small, dark ticket booth set to one

side. Sticking out of it and effectively barring their way was a huge, muscular, hairy arm. The arm bore a tattoo of a heart. Across the heart was the word MUDDER. It was the sort of arm you wouldn't want to argue with. The sort of arm only a Mudder could love.

'Ticket, please,' said a gravelly voice from the depths within. And the sausage-like fingers flapped with sluggish impatience.

'Derrrr . . . eh?' said Plugugly, taken aback.

'I said ticket, please,' repeated the arm's owner impatiently.

'Derrrrr . . . tick what? I don't get yer,' said Plugugly, confused, looking around for something to tick.

'You got to have a ticket,' explained the Arm. 'To get in.'

'No one ever said nuttin' about no tickets,' complained Plugugly, finally seeing the light. 'Did dey?' he appealed to the Goblins behind.

Everyone agreed that nobody had said anything about tickets. There was an anxious silence.

'So are you lettin' us in, den, or what?' asked Plugugly after a bit.

'Got any money?' asked the Arm.

A hasty trawl of the Goblins' pockets and back-packs produced quite a pile of interesting things. Ancient sweet wrappers. Crisp socks. A short, heavily knotted piece of old bootlace. A fossilized apple core. A safety-pin. The exhaust pipe off a motorbike. Part of an old mangle. Unpleasant handkerchiefs. Three rusty keys. A photograph of Sproggit's mum. Enough fluff to stuff a mattress. But money, sadly, was conspicuous by its absence.

'Can't we owe you?' asked Plugugly desperately.

'Nope,' said the Arm. 'You gotta have a ticket or you gotta gimme some dosh. Else you can clear orf.'

The Goblins simply couldn't take it in. They stared at the Arm blocking their way in slack-jawed disbelief. To suffer all that hardship, walk all those miles and then to be told to clear off? It was just too ghastly to contemplate.

It was Hog who finally broke the silence. He gave a shrill howl, threw himself full-length on the ground and began to pummel the grass with his fists. This was the cue for Slopbucket to stuff his knuckles in his eyes and start up a horrible wailing. Eyesore, Lardo and Stinkwart formed a circle and began to perform a dance which is known in Goblin circles as the Fed Up Stomp, and consists of stamping as hard as you can on someone else's foot while simultaneously pulling your hair, beating your breast and gnashing your teeth. (Ideally, it should be performed at full moon, but this was an emergency.)

Sproggit, with a shrill scream of frustration, ran at the tall fence which bordered Gobboworld and thumped it as hard as he could.

To his surprise, his arm went through.

''Ere!' hissed Sproggit. 'Over 'ere! Dis fence musta bin built by Goblins. Look, me arm's gone through! There's a 'ole!'

Sure enough, there was. A neat, fist-shaped one. Eagerly, Sproggit applied his eye to it. And oh, what sights he saw inside! It was enough to make a Goblin weep.

He saw the Bobble Hat of Doom – a great swing in the shape of an upturned bobble hat, full to the brim with laughing thrill-seekers. Even as he watched, it turned in a full circle, sending its shrieking passengers plummeting head-first into a large pool of warm, bubbling mud, which had been thoughtfully placed below.

He saw bungee-jumping with elastic that was

just that bit too long. He saw a roller-coaster with an interesting gap right at the top. He saw a helter-skelter which had been made even more exciting with the addition of a wall at the bottom. He saw . . .

'Less 'ave a decko, then,' complained Slopbucket, pulling at Sproggit's jumper. 'You've 'ad long enough, Sproggit. S'my turn now.'

'No it ain't, it's mine,' protested Hog. 'I was 'ere first.'

'No you wasn't! I was!' insisted Slopbucket, raising his voice.

'Oi!' boomed the voice of the Arm from the booth. 'You get away from that fence, you lot! Think I can't see you? Go on, clear orf. Shan't tell you again.'

'I wuz only looking,' whined Sproggit piteously, tearing his eye away with great reluctance. 'It's a free country.'

'Not in Gobboworld it ain't. See this arm?'

The fingers closed in a great, tight fist and the muscles wriggled ominously.

'Yeah?' said Plugugly, Hog, Lardo, Eyesore, Stinkwart, Slopbucket and Sproggit.

'Wanna see what it's attached to?'

The Goblins shook their heads. No. They didn't. They tore themselves away from the hole in the fence and stood in a subdued little cluster.

'Now what do we do?' Hog inquired brokenly.

'Go 'ome, I suppose,' said Lardo, kicking dully at a stone, which flipped up and hit Eyesore in the eye. Eyesore was so depressed he couldn't even be bothered to make a thing of it.

'I suppose we oughter look at de sea while we're here,' said Plugugly with a huge sigh.

'Why?' asked Slopbucket uninterestedly. 'What's so special about the sea? Nasty, big, grey, wet, sloppy thing, the sea. What we wanna look at that for?'

'I dunno,' said Plugugly with a shrug. 'Traditional, innit? Come to de seaside, gotta look at de sea. Anyway, you got any better ideas?'

Nobody had. So, muttering miserably, they trailed off towards the edge of the cliff.

And there they stood, hands in pockets, beside themselves with grief and disappointment, looking out over the heaving waves . . .

. . . on which bobbed a little boat. Or, rather, on which *sank* a little boat. Even as the Goblins watched, it gave up the unequal struggle and vanished beneath the surface, depositing its six passengers into the water.

But not before the Goblins recognized them. Oh dear me no. They knew those passengers all right.

'Boys,' said Plugugly, 'I reckon our luck's just turned.'

'Oh yeah? 'Ow's that, then, Plug?' asked Hog, watching the tragedy at sea with interest.

'Because,' said Plugugly slowly, 'because I got a nidear.'

CHAPTER TWENTY

A short while later, the Goblins once again stood at the ticket booth.

'You again,' said the Arm.

'Yep,' said Plugugly.

'Got yer tickets this time?' demanded the Arm with a sneer.

'Nope,' said Plugugly cheerfully. He had been through this little ritual before. He knew what to expect. He had all the right answers ready.

'Got any money?'

'Nope. We got summink better, ain't we, boys?'

'Yer!'

'Too right we 'ave!'

Excitedly, the Goblins agreed that they had indeed got something better. Something much, much better.

'Oh yeah? And what might that be?' the Arm asked with a sneer.

This was Plugugly's big moment.

'Step back, boys,' he commanded in ringing tones. 'Let 'im see de new Main Attraction!'

And the Goblins stood aside and the Arm got his first eyeful of the bedraggled, sorry-looking bunch that stood in an exhausted, dripping huddle behind them.

The captives glared back sullenly. It had been a long, hard swim to shore after the boat had capsized. Waves had buffeted them. Fish had nibbled them. Sharp rocks had grazed their knees. It was only due to the pockets of air trapped in Ronald's shorts (thus keeping them afloat) that they had made it at all.

Then, to add insult to injury, the minute they crawled thankfully on to dry land, they had fallen into enemy hands! To their great surprise and eternal shame, they had been pounced on by none other than Plugugly and Co., and tied up with a long, improvised rope consisting of Slopbucket's scarf, Lardo's braces and a heavily knotted fragment of Hog's old bootlace.

Pounced on! Tied up! By Goblins, of all things!

'It's embarrassing, that's what it is,' hissed Pongwiffy to Sharkadder through clenched teeth. She only normally took the one bath a year, and her sudden enforced dip in the briny had put her in a very bad mood indeed.

Sharkadder, busily squeezing water from her ruined hair, said nothing. But she glowered a great deal.

Lulu, who had quite spoiled her dress as well as losing her wig and one of her gold shoes, was weeping noisily – a sort of horrible lead singer caterwauling to which Ronald's chattering teeth provided a kind of castanet rhythm section.

Poor Ronald. Of all of them, he had suffered the worst. Being, as you might expect, an abysmally poor swimmer, he had swallowed a great deal of sea-water and looked as though he was shortly about to be very poorly indeed.

Both Hugo and Dudley were past caring. Their fur was plastered to their backs. Despite their tales of past daring exploits on the high seas, neither had proved to be a good swimmer. Both looked like exhausted water sacks and were too tired even to lick.

The sight of the sodden party obviously had an effect on the Arm. There came a startled gasp from the booth.

'Well, boil my bobble 'at! What you got there, then?'

'Told you,' said Plugugly, with pride. 'Amazin'

what de sea washes up. Two Witches, a Wizard in shorts, a Superstar an' a coupla cut-price Familiars. Not a bad catch, eh?'

It wasn't. For Goblins, who traditionally never caught anything, it was nothing short of miraculous.

''Old it right there,' said the Arm excitedly. 'I'll 'ave ter consult wiv my colleagues.'

And there came the sound of a door slamming, followed by the sound of rapidly disappearing footsteps.

The Goblins exchanged satisfied beams. Things really were looking up.

'D'you know what I could go for now?' remarked Hog. 'A nice, big, greasy plate o' chips. To celebrate.'

At this point, the sea-water in Ronald's stomach made a noisy reappearance.

'I'll get you for this, Plugugly,' snarled Pongwiffy, baring her teeth most unpleasantly. 'Just see if I don't.'

'Why? What you gonna do? Squelch us?' taunted Sproggit – a brilliantly witty remark which set the Goblins rocking with laughter.

'You can't put spells on us this time,' Slopbucket reminded her sneeringly. 'We ain't at 'ome now. There's a NO MAGIC rule in Sludgehaven, an' if you break it, we'll tell. So na, na, na, na, na!'

And he poked his tongue out and waggled his fingers on his nose, which was typical.

'I s-s-s-say!' said Ronald, who had suddenly found his voice. It had been lost for ages somewhere deep down in his stomach, along with the sea-water. And now, like the sea-water, it was back again!

'I say! You'd b-better jolly well loosen these b-b-bonds and let me go this minute. I'll have you know I'm a W-Wizard. I demand to be let go at once.'

'You're our 'ostage. You ain't going nowhere,' Hog told him cheerfully.

'That's right. We got plans fer you. Anyway, you can't do a fing wivout yer silly ole Wizard robes, can yer?' taunted Lardo.

'*A Wizard always needs 'is kit,*
Or else 'e can't do doodly-squit,' chanted Sproggit.
It was an old Goblin rhyme which all Goblins learn at their mother's knee. Unlike most old Goblin rhymes, it rang true.

'Is that true, Ronald? Can't you?' demanded Sharkadder.

Ronald flushed and bit his chattering lip. It was true. He couldn't. Wizardry depends on the paraphernalia. Without his Cloak of Darkness and his Hat of Knowledge and his Staff of Wisdom and whatnot, he was hopeless. Cold, too.

'Well, I must say, I'm very disappointed in you, after all that education,' said Sharkadder cuttingly. 'Just think. A nephew of mine. Can't even summon up a bit of lightning without his trousers on.

Tut tut. What *do* they teach in Wizard school these days?'

'Well, it's more the *theory* side of things . . . ' Ronald began desperately, but Pongwiffy stood on his foot and after a short squawk, he went quiet.

'Oi! Wizard! Let's see yer do a spell in them shorts!' jeered Hog, enjoying the comic potential of Ronald and not wishing to let it go.

''Ere! 'E could do a spell that makes everyone 'oo sees 'im laugh at 'im!' suggested Eyesore, adding, ''Ere! It's workin'!'

This made the Goblins so helpless with laughter that Pongwiffy almost considered suggesting they make a run for it. But she decided against it. After all, they were still tied up. In their current weakened state, they wouldn't get more than two paces without someone tripping up, and then they'd all fall down and be an even bigger laughing-stock than they were already.

'I fink we should apologize to de lady, though,' said Plugugly with a sudden show of gallantry. Lulu stopped bawling, and gave a hopeful sniff. 'Dat's Luscious Lulu Lamarre de Superstar, dat is. I seen 'er picture. 'Course, she ain't too luscious right now, but dat's cos she's all wet.'

Lulu began to snivel again.

'Dere, dere, don't you go gettin' all upset,' Plugugly said, patting her on the shoulder. 'We ain't got nuffin' against you. Come on, boys, show de lady dat Goblins got manners. Line up an take yer 'ats orf an' say yer sorry.'

Obediently, the Goblins lined up and solemnly said they were sorry. Lulu fluffed her hair and cheered up a bit, especially when Slopbucket confessed sheepishly that he was a big fan. 'But we can't let you go,' Plugugly explained sadly. 'You're part of de Main Attraction, see.'

'I'll give you Main Attraction!' snarled Pongwiffy, nearly bursting with fury. 'I'll zap you into next week, I will! I'll . . .'

'Naughty, naughty!' jeered Lardo, waggling his finger. 'The Rule. Remember?'

'I'll give you Rule . . . ' began Pongwiffy recklessly.

But luckily – or unluckily, as it turned out for some – at that moment, something happened. The music which had been continuously droning on in the background suddenly ceased. There was a silence – then a rumbling noise. Everyone turned to look at the great gates of Gobboworld, which gave a little shudder, opened a bit, stuck, then slowly, dramatically, drew apart.

'In yer go, then, sir,' said the Arm from the booth. 'I got instructions ter let yer pass.'

'Dis is it, den,' said Plugugly, swelling with pride. He'd never been called 'sir' before. 'Our big moment. Straighten up, you 'ostages. We're goin' in. Quick march. Er – 'ow's it go again?'

'Summink about right an' left, ain't it?' said

Hog, scratching his head.

'Das it! Right, 'ere we go. Right, right, left, right, right, left, er – left . . . '

And – somehow – in they went.

CHAPTER TWENTY-ONE

Back in Sludgehaven, blissfully unaware of the plight of their friends, the Witches were having the time of their lives. Bendyshanks, Ratsnappy and Sludgegooey were reclining in deckchairs on the promenade, busily writing postcards.

'*Dear Great-Aunt Grimelda*,' wrote Sludgegooey. '*Well, here we all are on our hols. It's all go. Yesterday we slimed a Punch and Judy Demon which was a right lark. Gaga's learnt to water-ski. Filth is getting quite a tan. Wish you were here. All the best, your loving niece, Sludgegooey.*'

'How d'you spell "disgusting"?' inquired Ratsnappy, sucking her pencil. 'I want to tell my cousin Catnippy about Old Molotoff's breakfasts,' she explained.

'How should I know? Ask Greymatter,' suggested Sludgegooey, sticking a stamp on.

'I daren't. She's still stuck on One Across. Here come the twins, look. Hey, you two! What's that you've caught?'

'Minnows,' said Agglebag proudly, showing her jam jar. 'Two of them. Twins, we think. We're taking them home, aren't we, Ag? To live happily ever after on our mantelpiece. We're calling them Minnie and Manfred.'

'How d'you know which is Manfred?' inquired Sludgegooey doubtfully.

'We don't yet,' confessed Bagaggle. 'But when we get home, Ag's going to knit him a little waterproof tie.'

'And Bag's going to make a little bow for Minnie,' agreed Bagaggle. 'We're good with our hands.'

This interesting conversation was interrupted by a further arrival. Scrofula and Macabre turned up with Barry and Rory in tow. They were all very excited, having found a little shop that sold sandwiches with decent, Witch-friendly fillings, including porridge.

'This is more like it,' said Macabre, parking herself in a deckchair and taking a huge bite of her porridge sandwich. 'This'll help make up for breakfast – or the lack of it. Anyone seen Bonidle?'

'Still in bed,' sighed Ratsnappy. She had the misfortune to be sharing a room with Bonidle, whose life was one long lie-in. 'I can't get her up. Cyril had to hoover under her this morning. Old Molotoff's quite put out about it.'

'What about Gaga?' someone else wanted to know.

'Scuba-diving,' said Scrofula.

There was a short silence. Nobody quite knew what scubas were, or why anyone should want to dive for them – but it sounded a Gaga-ish short of thing to do.

'Pongwiffy and Sharkadder still missing?' inquired Scrofula. A general nodding of heads signified that this was indeed the case. Nobody had seen them since breakfast.

'Ah well. Probably got tied up somewhere,' said Ratsnappy.

'Here comes Sourmuddle,' announced Macabre, pointing to an excited figure hurrying towards them with Snoop hard on her heels.

'Ah! There you are! We've been looking for you,' puffed Sourmuddle, waving a handful of little pink slips. 'I've got a lovely surprise for us all. My friend at the rifle range gave me all these free seats for this afternoon's Mystery Tour!'

Excited cries greeted this announcement. Everyone wanted to know what a Mystery Tour was.

'We all get on a coach and it takes us somewhere mysterious,' explained Sourmuddle.

'Where?' asked Macabre.

'If we knew that, Macabre, there wouldn't be a mystery, would there?'

'Supposing we don't like it when we get there?' objected Ratsnappy, who liked to be awkward.

'I shall demand a refund,' said Sourmuddle airily.

'I thought you said the seats were free?'

'So?' said Sourmuddle. 'I shall still demand a refund. I'm Grandwitch. I know my rights.'

So that was all right.

Meanwhile, up at the Magician's Retreat . . .

'I'm not at all sure about this Mystery Tour business, you know,' Arnold the Arsonist was saying. 'On a coach, do you say? Sounds a bit too adventurous for my liking. Will I be allowed to smoke, do you think?'

'Oh, I should think so,' said Dave the Druid, helping himself to another scone. 'We're Wizards, aren't we? Nobody tells us what to do.'

The Wizards were sitting in the lounge, tucking into lunch. Lunch, by popular request, was a cream tea set out on hostess trolleys. There were mountains of scones, vats of jam and great jugs of cream. There was much rattling of teacups and licking of fingers and greedy spooning of jam, which almost drowned out the sound of dry voices droning on in the Convention Room next door.

'Does it mean mixing with the riff-raff, though? That's what I want to know,' inquired Alf the Invisible anxiously. A scone laden with jam and cream rose from his plate, hovered a moment, then vanished in a puff of crumbs. Several of the crumbs remained hanging in mid-air, obviously caught on his invisible beard.

'Certainly not. I've spoken to the driver and arranged for us to be picked up first. We get the plum choice of seats,' explained Dave the Druid.

'That sounds very fair,' nodded Gerald the Just. But Alf the Invisible wasn't reassured.

'Why do we have to go anywhere? What's wrong with sitting on our balcony?'

'The maid wants to clean it,' explained Dave the Druid.

'But I thought we could start a little fire up there today,' mourned Arnold the Arsonist. 'I've got my magnifying glass all ready.'

'I just thought we should perhaps get out and about a little,' explained Dave the Druid. 'We don't have to move or anything. Just sit in a coach and watch the scenery go by. And I've arranged for the hotel to pack us up a hamper. Just a light snack. Couple of sides of ham, a cold chicken or two, some sandwiches, some tomatoes, a few eggs, pork pies, sausage rolls, a big cake, fizzy lemonade – that sort of thing. Just to keep us going until supper.'

'Oh well,' said Alf the Invisible, sounding relieved. 'If there's going to be a *hamper* . . .'

'I suppose we should let young Ronald read out his paper at some point,' said Frank the Foreteller, helping himself to his fourth scone. 'I could do with a good laugh.'

'Did anyone check his room, by the way?' asked Arnold the Arsonist. 'I don't think I've seen him all day, come to think of it.'

'Sulking, I shouldn't wonder,' said Frank the Foreteller with satisfaction, spooning on lashings of cream.

'Well, somebody had better tell him about the Mystery Tour,' said Dave the Druid. 'He wouldn't want to miss that. He's been complaining the whole time that we never do anything. Go on, Arnold. Pop up and give the lad his ticket.'

'Mmmm,' said Arnold vaguely. 'Later. After lunch. Er – does anyone want that last scone?'

Everyone did. So they ordered some more.

CHAPTER TWENTY-TWO

Scott Gets His Chance

Scott Sinister was in his dressing-room. In fact, he hadn't dared move from it since the previous day when he had run into Pongwiffy, of all people! Whatever was she doing in Sludgehaven? Wherever Pongwiffy went, trouble followed. He knew that. So what if she was the one remaining loyal fan he had left in the whole world? She was the sort of fan he could do without. Even on a hot day.

Scott gave a little shudder as he recalled that heart-stopping moment of the day before when they had come face to face. Luckily, he had escaped before she could engage him in conversation – or even worse – aaaah – kiss him!!?? One look at her dazzling smile of greeting had been enough for instinct to take over. He had uttered that low, rising, wobbling wail, taken to his heels and fled to the safety of his broom cupboard, where he spent the rest of the day and the whole of the night quaking under a pile of curtains, convinced she would seek him out.

But she hadn't. And now it was morning – and tonight was opening night. Scott was nothing if not a trouper. The theatre was in his veins. As his mum always boasted, his very first baby sentence (announced imperiously from the potty) had not been the usual 'I want my eggy.' It had been the far more impressive utterance, 'The show must go on.'

There was something about being in a theatre that aroused all the old actorly feelings. After all, tonight was opening night. The smell of old greasepaint, combined with the distant sounds of an orchestra tuning up, revived him as effectively as smelling-salts. Right now, he was sitting before his cracked mirror applying the finishing touches to his make-up. When he had finally got it to his satisfaction, he carefully combed his hair, took his sunglasses from his pocket and put them on.

There. That was an improvement. Time now for some soothing deep breathing. In – out – in – out.

The breathing helped a lot. In fact, he was beginning to feel much better. So much so that he felt ready to attempt his voice exercises.

'Mee mee meeeeeeee,' sang Scott. 'Mee mee mee ma mee moo may!'

There came the sound of pattering footsteps, followed by an urgent knock on the door.

'Who's in there, please?' came the voice of the Callboy.'

'Meeeeeeee!' trilled Scott.

'Is that you, Mr Sinister?'

'Of course it is,' snapped Scott. 'I'm trying to do my voice exercises. What do you want? I'm not receiving any visitors, mind.'

'You haven't got any, Mr Sinister. It's not that. It's Miss Lamarre. She's gone missing. Not in there with you, is she?'

'Of course not,' growled Scott. 'How can she be with me? There's only enough oxygen in here for one.'

'It's just that she's late for rehearsal. She was due here hours ago and she hasn't shown up. The orchestra's threatening to pack up and go home.'

'Well, what do you expect when you engage amateurs?' said Scott coldly. 'Kindly go away and leave me in peace. There are only a few hours to curtain-up. I want to be alone. I need to get into role.'

There was a short pause, and the footsteps pattered away.

Scott felt *much* better. Telling off the Callboy had made him feel more important, somehow. He could feel his old confidence flowing back. Perhaps he would go over his act one more time. He needed to be word perfect. His was only a small spot, but at least he'd give it all he'd got.

He fished inside his cloak, and brought out a sheaf of well-thumbed paper. He glanced briefly at the topmost sheet, mouthed a few words under his breath, then deliberately placed the script to one side, leaned back in his chair, closed his eyes and began.

'Thank you very much, ladies and gentlemen, thank you very much! Hey! It's great to be back in good old Sludgehaven again.' (Pause for applause. Hopefully.) 'Hey, I love the seaside, don't you? Talking of the sea, have you heard the one about the haddock who robbed a fish bar and was done for salt and battery? And what about the mermaid who . . .'

'Mr Sinister, sir!'

The Callboy was back again.

'What! What is it!' roared Scott. 'Can't an artiste be left to go over his lines in peace!'

'It's Miss Lamarre, sir. They still can't find her. The Stage Manager's going potty. He wants to know if you'll step into the breach.'

There was a startled silence. Then: 'Could you

just repeat that?' croaked Scott.

He couldn't believe he had heard aright. Surely it wasn't true! Could it be, could it *really* be that his luck had finally turned?

The Callboy took a deep breath.

'It's Miss Lamarre, sir. They still can't find her. The Stage Manager's going po . . .'

'Not the whole of it, idiot! Just the last bit. About stepping into the breach.'

'The Stage Manager wants you to go on in her place, sir. He's desperate. Every seat is sold for this evening's performance, and the star's missing. Will you do it, Mr Sinister? Will you save the show?'

Well. What would anyone say to a request like that?

For the first time for simply ages, a great smile spread across Scott's face. He stood, swept his cloak about him and pulled open the door with a flourish.

'Prepare the main dressing-room,' he said grandly. 'I am on my way.'

CHAPTER TWENTY-THREE

The Wizards were gathered in the foyer of the Magician's Retreat, waiting for the coach that was to take them on the Mystery Tour. They were all muffled up in case of draughts, and greedily eyeing the enormous hamper containing the light snack which was to fortify them during the excursion. All except the Venerable Harold, who had evidently found the excitement of a Mystery Tour too much to bear and had gone to sleep on a nearby sofa.

'Are we all here?' cried Dave the Druid, bustling about with a clipboard. Having organized the trip, he had taken it upon himself to be leader.

They were. All except Alf the Invisible, who couldn't strictly be described as *here*, although some floating crumbs and a smear of airborne cream indicated that he was present.

And Ronald, of course. (*We* know where he is, don't we? But they didn't.)

'I'm still not sure about this,' moaned Arnold the Arsonist through a cloud of thick grey smoke. He had got two pipes going at once, just in case Dave had been wrong and he wouldn't be allowed to smoke.

'Well, it's too late to change your mind now,' said Dave firmly. 'Here comes the coach.'

'Looks like young Ronald's going to miss all the excitement,' remarked Frank the Foreteller sadly. 'Shame, really.'

'No one bothered to check his room, I suppose?' inquired Dave the Druid. 'No? Oh well, too late now. Right, someone pass Harold to the front. We'll stick him in the back seat, along with the hamper.'

Down on the promenade, a large crowd of Witches and their Familiars were assembled by a sign that said THE MYSTERY TOUR, QUEUE HERE. The entire Coven was present, apart from Pongwiffy, Hugo, Sharkadder and Dudley. Even Bonidle and her Sloth had turned out of bed for this. Gaga was there too, all decked out in snorkel and flippers, carrying a large oil painting entitled

'The Minstrel Boy's Revenge', which she claimed to have won in a paragliding competition.

There was a great deal of excitement and much wild speculation about their possible destination.

'Ah hope it's Scotland,' said Macabre dreamily. 'Ah'll pop in for a decent bowl o' porridge wi' mah Uncle Fergus. Ah've brought mah bagpipes, just in case. He likes a wee tune.'

'I rather hope it's somewhere with a decent reference library,' groaned Greymatter, still doing battle with One Across. So far, she had worn out six pencils and thirteen dictionaries – but still the correct answer eluded her.

'Somewhere where you could get a decent hot meal would be a fine thing, wouldn't it, Ag?' remarked Bagaggle longingly.

'It would, Bag. Old Molotoff's starvation diet is getting on our nerves.'

This brought a chorus of heartfelt agreement from everybody.

'Hear hear!'

'Down with Old Molotoff and her rotten breakfasts, I say!'

'I sneaked a look over her shoulder into the larder this morning!' Bendyshanks informed everyone. 'Stuffed with pies and jelly and cake and stuff, it is. And all we get is eggs. Eggs, eggs, eggs.'

'Eggsactly!'

'What I can't understand is why Sourmuddle's

taking it all in her stride,' remarked Ratsnappy. 'She's always had a good appetite, has Sourmuddle. You'd think she'd be the first to complain.'

'What's that? Did I hear my name mentioned?' inquired Sourmuddle.

'We were just saying about the breakfasts,' explained Bendyshanks. 'We want to complain. We're all starving.'

'Really?' asked Sourmuddle. 'Snoop and I aren't. Are we, Snoop?'

'Ah,' said Snoop, 'but that's because . . .'

He caught Sourmuddle's eye and stopped abruptly in mid-sentence.

'That's because we're not greedy,' Sourmuddle finished off for him. 'I've told you before, it's not Done to complain about food. We're in a strange place with strange customs. When in Rome, do as the Romans do.'

'I bet the Romans got more to eat than boiled eggs,' complained Sludgegooey. 'In fact,' she went on, 'in fact, they got *loads* to eat. I heard that they got so much they couldn't eat it all, so they'd stick their fingers . . .'

Luckily, more information about the Romans' famous eating habits was prevented by the timely arrival of the coach.

'Hey!' shouted Bendyshanks, jumping up and down. 'It's here! Look! It says Mystery Tour on the front!'

'It's the same one that brought us! It's George, look! Bags I the back seat!'

'Wait a minute,' said Ratsnappy. 'I hate to put a damper on things – but aren't those *Wizards* I see?'

She was right. They were. A mass of bearded faces, incredulous with horror and topped with pointy hats, were pressed against the glass.

There was immediate consternation.

'Well, if anyone thinks I'm sharing a coach with a load of *Wizards* . . . '

'Look! They've got the best seats and all!'

'What a cheek. How come they get picked up first?'

'They've got a hamper too! Lucky blighters.'

Sourmuddle, as befitted her role of Grandwitch, reacted with dignity. It took more than a coachload of Wizards to unsettle her. Calmly, she picked up her skirts.

'Come along, girls, best foot forward. We're not going to let a few Wizards spoil our outing, are we? Open the door, George, we're coming in!'

The Wizards had indeed taken the best seats. The best seats were towards the back, away from the engine and the draughty door. They muttered and rumbled under their breath as the Witches and Familiars filed in and took their seats in sniffy silence.

'Pshaw! You see? Riff-raff! I told you!'

'If I'd known a load of *Witches* were coming on this trip . . . '

'They're bringing *animals* on, for goodness' sake. Is that a *haggis* they've got there? And are those *bats*, do you think?'

'Whatever is the world coming to?'

'There should be a law . . .'

Bendyshanks, who was the last one in, treated them all to a stony glare and plumped down heavily on Alf the Invisible's lap. They both howled with fright and Alf hastily fled to another seat.

'The air was all bony there for a moment,' explained Bendyshanks lamely in answer to the quizzical stares, and tentatively sat down again, looking quite shaken.

'Everyone in?' growled George. 'Right then. We're off.'

And with a shrill blast of the horn and an almighty grinding of gears, the coach lurched away.

There was a tense silence from both parties as they drove along the prom. It wasn't often that Wizards and Witches shared such a confined space. In the normal course of events, they avoided each other. If a Witch and a Wizard should pass each other on the street, they would stick their noses in the air and look the other way. They despised each other's Magical methods, for a start. With the Wizards, it was all lightning and colourful explosions, which the Witches considered flashy. They preferred cackling over cauldrons, a practice which the Wizards thought of as common.

For a while, nobody spoke. Then, suddenly, Sourmuddle spoke up.

'Is somebody smoking a smelly old pipe at the back there?' she demanded primly. 'If so, I'll thank you to put it out. We Witches have our own filthy habits. We don't have to put up with yours.'

Arnold the Arsonist gave a guilty start and looked around wildly, unsure of what to do.

'Don't you do it, Arnold,' advised Frank the Foreteller. 'You smoke as much as you like. Here, have a cigar. Have two.'

All things considered, it wasn't a wise move. In fact, it really set the cat among the pigeons.

'Boo! Put it out, put it out!' bellowed the Witches. 'Stop the coach! Make him put it out!'

'Don't do it, Arnold! You stand firm!' countered the Wizards. 'Keep going, driver, if you know what's good for you!'

'Open the windows! Open the windows!'

George sighed. It looked like it was going to be another of Those Days.

CHAPTER TWENTY-FOUR

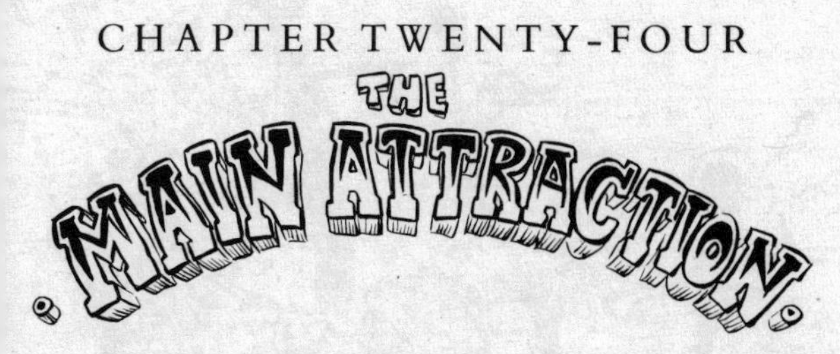

Meanwhile, back in Gobboworld a long, excited queue had formed for the popular Main Attraction. The Bobble Hat of Doom, the roller-coaster, the bungee jump and the helter-skelter lay idle. The various sideshows and stalls had all been abandoned in favour of this, the latest amusement, which was proving to be an absolute winner.

The Main Attraction had been hastily set up on a roped-off platform rather like a boxing ring. This was where the Goblins normally conducted their celebrated Wet Bobble Hat competitions – jolly occasions when particularly daft volunteers would stand grinning vacantly while eager crowds armed with long hoses attempted to squirt their hats off. That was a lot of fun, of course – but in terms of pure pleasure, it had nothing on this, the latest diversion, an absolute corker which really had them rolling in the aisles.

It was a Main Attraction that couldn't fail.

It was called Get Your Own Back, and consisted of *five* highly enjoyable, fun-filled activities. Hoop the Hag, Splodge the Wizard, Singalonga Superstar, Poke the Pet – and, for the grand finale –

Wash the Witch!

Sharkadder, Ronald, Lulu, Hugo, Dudley and Pongwiffy, bound hand and foot, stood in a grim-faced line while hordes of enthusiastic Goblins fought for the pleasure of throwing hoops at Sharkadder's nose (Hoop the Hag), hurling tomatoes at the hapless Ronald (Splodge the Wizard), singing interminable tuneless duets with Lulu (Singalonga Superstar), tickling Hugo and Dudley with feathers tied on the end of long poles until they begged for mercy (Poke the Pet), and last – and best of all – setting upon Pongwiffy armed with a bucket of warm water, a large sponge and a huge bar of pink soap! (Wash the Witch. What else?)

Warm water! Soap! Pongwiffy! Can you imagine?

'Roll up, roll up!' shouted Plugugly through a megaphone, banging on a bucket containing an unpleasant mess of overripe tomatoes. Below him, Eyesore, Lardo, Slopbucket, Hog and Sproggit moved among the crowds, distributing hoops, tickling sticks, sponges, and buckets of warm, soapy water. 'Dis way fer de Main Attraction! Step right up, ladies an' gennelmen. Chance of a lifetime! Get Yer Own Back fer a change!'

Nobody needed any coaxing.

'I suppose they think this is funny,' ground out Sharkadder between clenched teeth. Cheers rang out as a fourth hoop rattled on to her nose, neatly lining up with three others which had already met their mark. 'Hoop the Hag indeed! I've never been so insulted in my life. Some holiday this is turning out to be. Ouch! That hurt!'

'Grooo,' said Ronald through a mouth full of tomatoes. He had always hated tomatoes. They were in his hair too. Pulpy juice trickled into his ears and dripped on to his thin shoulders. Even his nice yellow shorts were getting stained. It was a high price to pay for a paddle.

Next along, Lulu was singing. Singalonga Superstar was proving to be an inspired idea. Goblins enjoy a good sing-song, and it wasn't often they got the chance to warble along with someone as famous as Luscious Lulu Lamarre. One by one, grinning sheepishly, they filed on to the platform and whispered their requests into her ear. Once Lulu had kicked off, they mumbled along tunelessly while their friends cheered and whistled and took photographs. 'Oh I Do Like to be Beside the Seaside' was a popular one, closely followed by 'My Way'.

'I'm not singing any more,' Lulu had complained at one point, stamping her foot petulantly. 'My throat hurts.'

'Fair enough. You can give out kisses instead if you like,' offered Slopbucket with a hopeful giggle and going all pink.

'Oh, I do like to be beside the seaside . . . ' trilled Lulu quickly.

Compared with the other victims, Hugo and Dudley had it easy. After all, they were only being tickled. But, as Hugo said later, it's no fun being tickled by your sworn enemies.

Of all of them, though, Pongwiffy suffered the most. Coming into contact with soap was her worst ever nightmare and the Goblins knew it. My, how they applied themselves! How they rubbed and scrubbed and lathered and mopped! There was lather in her eyes and up her nose. She could hardly be seen for foam. The sea had been bad enough, but this! This was without doubt the greatest indignity she had ever suffered.

'You'll be sorry!' she spluttered through a mouthful of froth. 'I'll get you for this, you see if I don't! Oi! Plugugly! Sproggit! You wait till we get back to Witchway Wood! I'll pulverize you! I'll turn you all into creepy-crawlies and make you live under my stove! I'll turn you into bedbugs and make you live under my mattress. I'll . . .'

But another grinning Goblin was approaching with the foaming sponge, and the rest of her threats were drowned out.

'There's only one good thing about this,' remarked Sharkadder as another hoop landed on her beringed nose with a clang.

'What's that, Auntie?' choked Ronald, by now as near to a bottle of ketchup as it is possible for a human to be.

'At least none of the others is here to see this,' groaned Sharkadder. 'We'd never live it down!'

'I beg your pardon, driver?' said Sourmuddle. 'Could you just repeat that? For a moment I thought you said we were here.'

'We are,' said George, switching off his engine and pulling open the door. 'This is it. End o' the Mystery Tour.'

'Do correct me if I'm wrong,' said Sourmuddle politely, 'but I believe that sign over those big gates says Gobboworld.'

'That's right,' said George. 'In you go. You got one hour to enjoy yourselves. Then I'm leavin'.'

There was a shocked silence from both Witches and Wizards alike. Nobody moved.

'Go on, then,' urged George. 'Out you get. You can't stop in the coach. Safety regulations.'

'You mean this is *it*?' demanded Arnold the Arsonist from the back. 'You stuck us in with a coachload of common Witches who won't even let a man *smoke* and brought us all that way for *this*?'

This brought mutters of protest from the Witches, along the lines of 'Hear that? Who's he calling common?' and so on.

'Why, what's wrong with it?' argued George defensively. 'Thought yer'd like to visit Gobbo-world. Somethin' a bit different, innit?'

There was an instant outcry.

'Well I never!' said Bendyshanks, disgusted. 'What a swiz!'

'And tae think ah thought it was Scotland!' wailed Macabre as her vision of a hot bowl of porridge poured itself away. Rory laid a sympathetic hoof on her lap.

'Disgraceful!' huffed and puffed the Wizards, equally put out.

'Outrageous! Shouldn't be allowed!'

'Some Mystery Tour! The only mystery is why we ever came on it!'

'Well, I for one will certainly be demanding a refund,' said Sourmuddle crossly. With a sigh, she stood up and reached for her handbag. 'Oh well. Come on, girls. Now we're here, we might as well take a look, I suppose. There's nothing else to do. Unless, of course, our esteemed fellow passengers would like to share the contents of that greedy-looking hamper with us.'

'Dream on!' shouted the Wizards. 'The hamper's ours!'

The Wizards were smarting. To their eternal shame, they had lost the battle of the pipe. Ratsnappy had simply marched up the aisle to where Arnold the Arsonist sat, snatched away his pipes, cigars, tobacco pouch and box of matches and thrown them out of the window.

It had been an embarrassing defeat. It had made the Wizards all the more determined to defend their hamper against all comers.

'So are we getting out or what?' inquired Arnold the Arsonist, fumbling in a secret pocket for the emergency pipe he kept there. 'I'm for a smoke myself.'

'I think we'd better,' agreed Gerald the Just. 'We might as well get our money's worth. Besides, I'm sure our driver could do with a break,' he added fairly.

'You're tellin' me,' said George.

'But what about the hamper?' came the anxious chorus. 'Will it be safe?'

'I'll lock it in the coach,' promised George. 'Out you get, then, gents. Only an hour, mind, then back 'ere sharp. I got a schedule to keep.'

With a great deal of sighing and complaining and creaking and casting about for scarves and woolly mufflers and suchlike, the Wizards filed from the coach and shuffled off to catch up with the Witches, who were marching in a determined crocodile towards the ticket booth.

CHAPTER TWENTY-FIVE

THE RESCUE

The Arm saw them coming and quailed. One minute everything was nice and quiet, the next its cosy little world was turned upside-down, along with the cup of tea it was currently enjoying.

Witches!?

Wizards!!??

Together???!!!

Ulp.

Whatever were they doing here? Could it be – horrors! – could it be that this was a properly organized rescue party who had somehow found out about the new Main Attraction and was coming to take revenge? The sight of so many pointy hats was truly frightening and it gave the Arm a real turn.

Lesser arms would have immediately retreated in alarm and reappeared holding a white flag. Not this Arm. This Arm was a pro. It set down its empty teacup, then stuck out again, effectively blocking the entrance. Granted it was shaking a little and its thick black hairs stood up on end – but to its credit, it held firm. Its mudder would have been proud.

'Open the gates up, if you please,' demanded Sourmuddle briskly. 'I've got a party of Witches here on a Mystery Tour. We've come to look at Gobboworld. Not our choice, you understand, but now we're here we might as well.'

'Oh, you don't want to go in *there*,' gibbered the Arm. 'You wouldn't like it. Not your sort of thing at all.'

'How do you know?' snapped Sourmuddle. 'You haven't a clue about what Witches like. Now open up before I get annoyed.'

'Anyway,' added the Arm hopefully, 'anyway, we're closed.'

'Oh yes? What's all that cheering I can hear coming from inside, then?'

'I meant full,' amended the Arm. 'That's it. We're full. An' anyway, it's private. Only Goblins allowed.'

'Enough of this nonsense!'

Dave the Druid bustled impatiently to the front. 'Stand aside, Sourmuddle, I'll deal with this. Come along, man, come along! We Wizards haven't got all day. We've got a Conference to attend.'

'Hear hear! Quite right. You tell him,' rumbled the Wizards supportively.

'I need ter see yer tickets,' pleaded the Arm.

'Tickets schmickets,' snapped Sourmuddle. 'Since when have Witches needed tickets? Now hurry up and open those gates. You don't keep Witches waiting.'

'Or Wizards,' poked in Dave the Druid.

'Well, I dunno . . . ' muttered the Arm. 'I got my instructions, see. Nobody's allowed to enter without a tick . . . *ow!*'

It broke off with a sharp cry of pain as Sourmuddle smacked it. Hard, right on the back of the wrist. Hastily it withdrew into the booth.

'Something wrong with your ears?' inquired Sourmuddle. 'When a Witch tells you to do something, you do it. Naughty boys who don't listen to Witches get smacks. Now. Open those gates this minute. Or do you want another one?'

The Arm didn't want another one. Without any more argument, it pressed the button that opened the gates.

Inside, Get Your Own Back was still doing record business. There was no doubt about it. It was proving to be the high spot of Gobboworld. There wasn't a Goblin there who didn't want to have a go.

The queuing system had long since broken down. A baying rabble now clustered thickly around the platform, pushing and shoving and howling with impatience. Some of the bigger ones had already had two turns, to the annoyance of some of the smaller ones who had been waiting for ages.

One such Goblin was right at the back of the milling crowd. His name was Squit. And it was because he was right at the back that he was the only one who heard the main gates rumble open behind him. Squit glanced back over his shoulder – and saw a sight that made him do a double take, then go weak at the knees.

'Oooer,' said Squit. 'Er – boys? *Boys!* I think we got visitors.'

And indeed they had.

Just inside the gates, the coach party stood in a tableau of frozen disbelief. Their mouths hung open and their eyes boggled at the scene before them.

'Witches!' squawked Squit, beating frantically on the wall of backs. 'Witches and Wizards, *'undreds* of 'em! Look to yer rear! Emergency, emergency! We bin rumbled!'

The word went round like wildfire. Well, actually, it didn't. Goblins are slow to cotton on, and it was more like a damp squib on a slow fuse. Eventually, though, the message filtered through. *The Witches* were here! *With the Wizards!*

Slowly, the cheers and catcalls died away. Hoops were guiltily lowered. Tomatoes were hastily stuffed into pockets. Tickling sticks were hidden. Soapy sponges were abandoned. The crowd parted, peeling back on two sides and providing a clear pathway that led from the platform back to where the unexpected visitors stood in shocked disbelief.

'Uh-oh,' said Plugugly sadly. 'Dat's us done for, den. Caught in de act. Goo'bye, cruel world.'

Up on the platform, aware of the sudden silence that had fallen, the six wretched captives raised abject eyes and stared at their rescuers with a mixture of relief and shame. Relief that their ordeal was over. Shame that they should be discovered in such embarrassing circumstances.

'I'm not seeing things, am I? That *is* Pongwiffy up there, under all that soap?' asked Sourmuddle, finally finding her voice. She sounded doubtful. It was hard to recognize Pongwiffy without her customary layers of grime.

'It certainly looks like it, Sourmuddle,' agreed Macabre grimly. 'What a turn-up, eh?'

'What's Sharkadder doing with all those rings on her nose, do you think, Ag?' asked Bagaggle, sounding puzzled. 'Is she doing an impression of a curtain rail, or what?'

'Possibly, Bag. And isn't that Lulu Lamarre the Superstar? What's *she* doing?'

Consternation was also running through the ranks of the Wizards.

'Are my eyes deceiving me, or is that young Ronald up on that platform?' quavered Harold the Hoodwinker, sounding puzzled. 'All covered in tomatoes, isn't he? And where are his trousers? Not very dignified, is it?'

'I'm afraid you're right, Harold,' confirmed Frank the Foreteller gleefully. 'Dearie dearie me. Looks like the lad's made a bit of a laughing-stock of himself, don't you think? Got himself in another pickle. Or should I say chutney, ha ha? *Tomato* chutney, I meant. Get it?'

'Letting the side down, I call it,' tutted Alf the Invisible. 'A very poor show indeed.'

'Of course, it's probably all the Goblins' fault,' said Gerald the Just fairly.

'True,' chorused all the Witches and Wizards together, then looked at each other in surprise. It

wasn't often they found themselves in agreement.

'How long did the driver say we've got?' Sourmuddle asked Dave the Druid, beginning to roll up her sleeves.

'One hour,' Dave told her.

'Excellent. That should be plenty of time. I think this calls for a bit of united action, don't you? A temporary truce. All for one and one for all. Agreed?'

'Agreed,' nodded Dave. 'Just this once, mind.'

'Right. Let's teach these Goblins a lesson they won't forget. Ready, everyone?'

'Ready!' came the chorus from Witches and Wizards alike.

'*Then let's get 'em!*'

And the Goblins scattered, screaming, in all directions, as the rescue party charged.

CHAPTER TWENTY-SIX

A Triumphant Return

What a different atmosphere there was in the coach as it wended its way back towards Sludgehaven that evening. Instead of argument, there was laughter and singing. Instead of bickering, there was hearty back-slapping and self-congratulation, particularly among the Wizards, who weren't used to physical exercise. Reducing Gobboworld to a pile of smoking rubble had proved to be a lot more strenuous than shuffling between bed and dinner table – but by golly, it had been fun! In fact, it had been a real tonic. Even the Venerable Harold the Hoodwinker looked ten years younger. Well, five, maybe.

'We showed 'em, didn't we?' shouted Arnold the Arsonist, dropping ash all down his front. 'We knocked the spots off those Goblins! They won't mess with Wizards again in a hurry. Did you see my karate jabs? Aaiiiiii – ha!'

'What about me, then?' piped up Harold the Hoodwinker in his quavering little voice. 'Did you see me wallop that big one? Thwack, right on his nose! Didn't think I still had it in me.'

'But did you see *me* when I took over the hose?'

crowed Frank the Foreteller, flushed with triumph. 'I made 'em run all right!'

'Ah, but you should have seen when I chased a great gang of 'em into the mud pool! Terrified, they were!'

'Terrified? You want to see terrified, you should have seen the one I chased up the roller-coaster, white as a sheet he was. You see, the way it happened was like this . . .'

'And it was fair too,' Gerald the Just was saying. 'That's what I like about it. We didn't use the unfair advantage of Magic. We beat them fair and square, and that's all there is to it.'

'What a day, eh?' sighed Dave the Druid. 'Almost worth young Ronald getting captured for. What d'you say, young Ronald? Feeling any better yet?'

Ronald, wrapped in a blanket, stared out of the window and said nothing.

'I say we break open the hamper,' suggested Frank the Foreteller. 'I reckon young Ronald here would like a bite to eat. What about it, lad? Fancy a nice *tomato* sandwich, ha ha ha?'

Ronald picked pips from his hair and continued to say nothing.

'There, there,' Gerald the Just consoled him. 'Don't take it to heart. I'm sure we all made fools of ourselves in our youth. Tell you what. We'll take you back to the hotel and clean you up, then order a whacking great six-course celebratory dinner. Then tomorrow we'll all come and hear you read out your paper at the Convention. Now I can't say fairer than that, can I?'

Ronald cheered up a bit.

The Witches too were all in excellent humour. There was nothing like wiping the floor with Goblins to put them in a good mood. All, that is, except Pongwiffy and Sharkadder. They weren't in a good mood at all. Bedraggled, bruised and humiliated, they sat slumped soggily together in the front seat with Dudley and Hugo on their laps, stonily ignoring various gibes along the lines of 'Who got caught by Goblins, then?' and 'Been starring in a soap, Pongwiffy?' and other such staggeringly witty comments.

It was no fun, being the butt of everyone's jokes.

'Hear that?' muttered Pongwiffy to Sharkadder as yet another chorus of 'I'm Forever Throwing

Goblins' started up. 'It's all very well for them. They haven't suffered like I have. Look at me! I'm all *pink*! It'll take weeks to get back to normal. Yuck.'

'You? *You?* What about me? Have you seen my *hair*? I've never been so embarrassed in all my life. I've become a complete laughing-stock, and it's all your fault, Pongwiffy, and I'll never forgive you. You've completely ruined my holiday.'

'Well, I like that!' said Pongwiffy, hurt. 'I was only trying to help Scott. At least that part of the plan worked. We got *her* out of the way, didn't we?'

She fired off a look of dislike at Lulu, who was sitting in tight-lipped silence next to George at the very front. She was being given a lift back to Sludgehaven at the Wizards' gallant insistence. The Witches were in far too frisky a mood to care one way or the other.

'At least Scott got his chance,' Pongwiffy went on. 'The show should be ending round about now. Oh, how I wish we'd been there to see it. I just *know* he'll have been a success. Just imagine it, Sharky. Our very own Scott's name back up in lights and all thanks to me. It'll make all our suffering worthwhile, won't it?'

'No,' said Sharkadder bitterly. 'Nothing could make up for what Dudley and I have been through today. Except perhaps a huge, greedy supper. But we won't get that at old Molotoff's.'

Outside, evening had fallen. The coach wheezed its way to the top of the last hill. A pale moon floated in the dark sky, lighting up the big welcoming sign that read: YOU ARE APPROACHING SLUDGEHAVEN. MAGIC STRICTLY FORBIDDEN. The lights of Sludgehaven glimmered below. From here, the distant pier looked like fairyland.

Cheers broke out, accompanied by the unmistakable sound of corks popping from bottles of celebratory fizzy lemonade. The Wizards had broken open the hamper, and were busily passing around chicken legs and sausage rolls.

'Well, come on then,' shouted Sludgegooey. 'Pass a few down to the front. Don't keep 'em all to yourselves. There's a lot of hungry Witches down here. Give us a sandwich, you greedy blighters.'

'Not jolly likely,' crowed the Wizards. 'Get your own sandwiches.'

'I thought we had a truce,' Sourmuddle reminded them. 'One for all and all for one. United we stand, united we fall, remember?'

'That was Goblins. This is food,' explained Dave the Druid through a mouthful of chocolate cake. 'With food, it's Every Wizard for Himself. Sorry.'

'Well I'm jiggered!' grumbled Sourmuddle, disgusted. 'There's Wizards for you.'

Down in Sludgehaven, crowds of excitedly chattering theatregoers streamed back along the pier, away from the Pavilion, where they had just been enjoying what had been, by common consensus, *the best show they had seen in a very long time!*

For Scott, it had been a charmed night. The sort of night of which every actor dreams. One of those wonderful, enchanted evenings when everything for once had gone right.

His make-up had gone on like a dream, and when he changed into his stage gear of top hat and tails, the tea lady slipped him a Jammy Dodger at no extra charge and told him he looked quite the toff.

The coffee machine in the proper dressing-room worked. The stage hands addressed him politely, patting him on the back and saying 'Good luck, Mr Sinister, we know you can do it' and

'We're all behind you, Mr Sinister', and encouraging things like that. When he stood waiting in the wings, listening to the warm murmuring of the audience out front, he felt ready for anything. His luck had turned. He could feel it in his bones. He couldn't wait to get out there and do his stuff!

The lights had dimmed on cue. The overture had started on time. The curtains hadn't stuck. When he had come running gaily on stage, he hadn't tripped over. His joke about the haddock was greeted with uproarious laughter. He had remembered the words of the songs and managed to stay almost in tune. When he sat on a stool in the spotlight and sang a particularly drippy love song, several female Trolls and an entire clutch of Banshees wept so much they were politely asked to leave.

His tap-dancing routine had gone down a treat – never had his feet skipped so lightly or his legs kicked so high. He had even managed to do the splits without rupturing either himself or his trousers, which takes real talent, as anyone in show business will tell you.

Throughout his entire performance, the audience had been on the edge of their seats, hanging on his every word, laughing, clapping, joining in with the songs, roaring for more. At the end, they had given him a standing ovation and made him come back on to take bow after bow after bow.

Backstage, after the show, his dressing-room

had bulged with flowers, chocolates and messages of congratulation. The Stage Manager had pumped his hand up and down and trebled his salary on the spot. Well-wishers filed in and out, telling him he was the tops and how they had always secretly preferred him to Lulu Lamarre and asking him when his next film was coming out.

And now, with the sound of clapping still ringing in his ears, he stood on the top step of the theatre with the night breeze cooling the sweat on his brow, shaking hands, signing autographs for fans and posing for pictures, murmuring 'Thank you, luvvies' and 'You're too kind, darlings', just like he always used to before his slide into oblivion. Mmmm. The sweet smell of success. How he had missed it.

He didn't notice the scruffy coach that squealed to a sudden halt at the end of the pier. He didn't notice the wild-eyed creature with tangled locks and a torn pink gown and one gold shoe who threw herself down the steps and came stumbling towards him along the pier. He didn't notice until she hurled herself into his arms with a shrill squawk.

'Scott! Oh, Scott, it's me! Am I too late? Have I missed the show?'

He staggered backwards and almost missed his footing – but didn't. Tonight was his night and nothing could go wrong.

'Lulu!' he cried, recovering his balance.

'Whatever can have happened to you? You look simply dreadful.'

'It was those old Witches again,' sobbed Lulu. 'They tricked me, Scott! They pretended to be rich producers and old boatmen and then the dead fish came alive but it wasn't really it was them and there was a horrible cat and a sick hamster and they put me in a boat and made me sit next to a wet Wizard in shorts and then the boat capsized and I had to swim to shore and then some horrid Goblins came along and tied us all up and made me sing and then – '

'Darling,' said Scott gently. 'My poor, hysterical darling, get a hold of yourself. This sounds like the far-fetched plot of some very silly book. You've been working too hard, precious. None of this happened, sweetheart. It's all been a terrible dream. You need a nice rest away from the public eye for a while.'

'But . . .'

'No buts, angel. It's tough at the top. It takes grit as well as talent. It's obvious you can't take the pace. Besides,' he added, trying not to sound too pleased, 'besides, you've been fired.'

Lulu burst into loud sobs.

'There there,' Scott soothed her, patting her back. 'Never fear. Scotty will take care of you. And in a couple of years, when you're back on your feet again, you never know – maybe I'll offer you a bit part in my next movie.'

'Oh, Scott! Scott! Boo-hoo! I've missed you, Scott.'

'And I've missed you too, Lulu, darling.'

Back in the coach, Pongwiffy, Hugo, Sharkadder and Dudley surveyed the tender scene with disgusted eyes.

'Well, there's gratitude!' said Pongwiffy. 'Look at 'em! All lovey-dovey. It's enough to make you sick. That's the last time I save *his* career.'

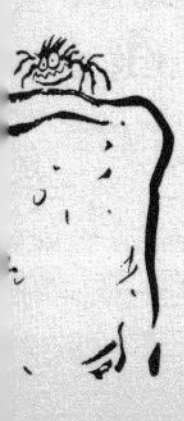

CHAPTER TWENTY-SEVEN

No Feast for the Wicked

'And what time of night do you call *this*?' demanded Mrs Molotoff. She was standing in the doorway in dressing-gown and slippers and with her hair in paper curlers, having been aroused from bed by a thunderous knocking at the door, accompanied by rowdy singing.

'Supper time,' Sourmuddle told her briskly.

'*Supper?* At this time of night? How dare you!' squawked Mrs Molotoff, bristling with fury. 'I told you, this is a respectable guest house. You have to obey the rules.'

'Well, that's just where you're wrong,' said Sourmuddle stoutly, to everyone's surprise. 'I'm Grandwitch and I do what I like.'

The Witches murmured excitedly among themselves as their noble leader marched up the steps, took a firm handful of dressing-gown, and placed her nose squarely within one inch of Mrs Molotoff's.

Could this be a showdown?

'Listen here, you old skinflint, and listen good,' hissed Sourmuddle. 'I've just about had enough of you. I've got a party of ravenous Witches here.

We've just returned from a highly successful rescue mission, and we're in a party mood, see? And what we'd like right now is some proper food. I'm not talking eggs, mind. I'm talking cold turkey and raspberry jelly and sherry trifle and chocolate biscuits and little-sausages-on-sticks. And some of that nice fruit cake you keep in the tin on the top shelf. In fact, I'm talking a major *feast*, understand? So why don't you just toddle on into the kitchen and make a start, eh? Else I just might lose my temper and do something nasty. I'm going to count to three. One . . .'

'This is intolerable!' spluttered Mrs Molotoff. 'The House Rules clearly say No Feasts.'

'Bother the House Rules,' said Sourmuddle. 'Two.' Little sparks were beginning to fizz at her fingertips. Mrs Molotoff went pale.

'You're not allowed to do that! There's a No Magic law in Sludgehaven . . . '

'Bother the law. Three.'

She muttered briefly under her breath, twiddled her fingers and, with a blinding flash, Mrs Molotoff disappeared! Her dressing-gown and slippers were still there, and a neat little pile of screwed-up papers – but she had gone.

In her place squatted a small, surprised-looking chicken. It blinked once or twice at the shocked company and gave a couple of angry clucks. Then, suddenly, its spindly legs crossed, a desperate expression came over its face and it headed for the nearest bush at a run.

'Oooooh,' gasped the Witches. 'Now you've done it, Sourmuddle! You used Magic! You turned Mrs Molotoff into a chicken!'

'That's right,' said Sourmuddle cheerfully. 'I rather think she's gone to lay an egg.'

'Hooray!' yelled the Witches. 'Good old Sourmuddle!'

'Actually,' added Sourmuddle, with a little chuckle, 'actually, girls, I've got a confession to make.'

She rummaged deep in her handbag, and brought out something that everyone instantly recognized.

'It's the larder key,' confessed Sourmuddle. 'Or, rather, a copy. I pinched the real one when old Molotoff wasn't looking and had a duplicate made. Snoop and I have been sneaking down at night and helping ourselves. We've enjoyed quite a few midnight feasts, haven't we, Snoop?'

'Well, I never!' gasped the Witches, torn between disgust and admiration. 'You old dark horse, you!'

'You mean we've been going hungry all this time and you and Snoop have been busily stuffing yourself behind our backs?' cried Ratsnappy. 'Well, if that doesn't take the cake!'

'Tee hee hee,' tittered Sourmuddle, obviously delighted with herself. 'I took the cake all right. Sneaky, aren't I? Sneaky and crafty and underhand. Which is why I'm Top Witch and you lot are still milling about in the ranks. Am I right?'

Ruefully, the Witches nodded. She was right.

'Anyway, enough of all this chat,' cried Sourmuddle. 'Come on, girls, in we go. Someone wake Cyril up and stick him in the kitchen with an apron on. It's party time!'

CHAPTER TWENTY-EIGHT

Like all good holidays, the last few days flashed by at the speed of light. Most of the time was taken up with the traditional holiday pursuits of sun-bathing, eating, paddling, fishing, eating, sleeping, eating and clock golf. Of course, quite a few interesting things happened too.

There was a visit from the man from the council, who had somehow got to hear that a certain Coven of Witches had been using Magic, which of course was strictly against the law.

Sourmuddle remarked that, while of course she saw his point, she would remind him that her girls had been mainly responsible for the total decimation of Gobboworld, for which the residents of Sludgehaven should be eternally grateful. She followed this up by asking him mildly whether he'd spent much time as a slug recently? The man from the council saw her point too, and agreed to drop charges.

There was the highly successful Coven outing to see the born-again superstar Scott Sinister starring in the Summer Spektacular, which Pongwiffy and her fellow hostages sniffily refused to attend on principle. After all, as Hugo was heard to remark, 'Zere is such a sink as pride.'

There was the time when Gaga went snorkelling in her pointy hat and got mistaken for a shark, causing the entire beach to be evacuated.

There was the memorable occasion when Sharkadder visited the Hall of Mirrors for the first time and fell in a dead faint at the sight of her greatly magnified peeling nose.

There was the wonderful moment when Greymatter finally saw the light and answered One Across. *Words spoken by backward giant (3,2,2,3).* Answer: Fum Fo Fi Fee.

Then, of course, there was the time the Brooms, bored silly with hanging around in a shed, broke out and went skinny-dipping at midnight. And the night when Sharkadder's hedgehog hair rollers got loose and ended up in Bonidle's bed. Then there was the occasion when Macabre got into a row with two Mummies about sunbeds and . . .

Well, you get the picture. Suffice it to say that the Witches had a whale of a time. This included Pongwiffy, whose many talents include a wonderful ability to bounce back. In no time at all, she got over the business with Scott Sinister and Lulu and was able to put the horrible experience of being washed by Goblins behind her. Much to her delight, her customary dirt soon began to build up. In fact, it must be said that, by the end of the celebratory feast, she was quite a good way towards being her old self again.

The Wizards had their moments too. Such as the one when Alf the Invisible fell over the balcony and nobody noticed. And that terrible time when the hotel ran out of greasy sausages. And Black Wednesday, when they realized they had posted their postcards without putting any stamps on and would have to do them all over again.

And what of Ronald? Well, depending on what

you think of him, you will be either pleased or disappointed to hear that (at Gerald the Just's insistence) he finally got the chance to read out his paper. His four-hour-long address on the subject of pointy hats went down in Convention history as the only speech ever to empty the hall. After the first ten minutes, even the hardened Convention-goers, the ones with the briefcases and the serious beards, were begging to be allowed to go for a drink of water and were not coming back.

It won a prize, of course, and got published in an obscure Wizardly journal. And that cheered Ronald up enormously. From that moment on, he decided never to go paddling again, but to concentrate on his studies instead. Sadly, it didn't do him any good. Among his fellow Wizards, he was never taken seriously and was always referred to disparagingly as 'Ronald the Paddler' instead of Ronald the Magnificent, which is what he would have liked to be called. And to this day he hasn't got a chair. Or a locker.

But for four long hours, it did his ego a bit of good.

Mrs Molotoff remained a chicken for the duration of the holiday. When the spell wore off and she finally returned to normal, conditions improved at Ocean View. She wasn't so inclined to henpeck Cyril. She'd had enough henpecking to last her a lifetime.

Also, she found she had gone right off eggs. She

wouldn't have an egg in the house. At the very mention of the word, she would give a little wince and have to go and lie down in a darkened room.

But that was later, after the Witches had left.

On the night of departure, they assembled sadly in the front garden with their Familiars, their luggage and their Brooms. They had decided to fly back to Witchway Wood – mainly because George had put his foot down and refused to drive them, but also because they fancied the idea. The weather conditions were perfect, with a big yellow moon hanging in the sky. The Brooms champed at their bits, eager to be off.

From inside Ocean View, there came the sound of a Hoover as Cyril began the big clear-up.

There was a lot of fussing about with string and rope and elastic bands as people attempted to fit five-feet-wide trunks on to one-inch-wide pieces of stick. And that was without all the extra bits and pieces they had collected! The shells, the interesting pebbles, the dried seaweed, Minnie and Manfred, the straw hats, Sourmuddle's goldfish, the sticks of rock, Gaga's oil painting, Mr Punch's nose, the towel from the bathroom, the . . . Well. You know the sort of thing.

'Are we all ready then?' said Sourmuddle. 'Did anyone remember to give a tip to Cyril? Those were pretty good breakfasts he cooked.'

'Aye,' said Macabre. 'I gave him a tip. I told him to put more salt in the porridge.'

'That's all right then. Right, everyone, this is it. End of holiday. Back to Witchway Wood and the humdrum round of cackling over cauldrons and trudging around wet fields looking for spotty toadstools in the fog.'

'And trying to buy non-existent ingredients in Malpractiss Magic Inc.,' said Sludgegooey.

'And the Friday night Coven meetings,' Macabre reminded them. 'Don't forget them.'

'And the brews,' chipped in Bendyshanks.

'And writing seriously good poetry,' added Greymatter.

'And playing our violins,' chorused Agglebag and Bagaggle.

'And washing my hair,' supplied Scrofula.

'And sleeping in my own little bed,' yawned Bonidle.

'And watching Gaga loop the loop over a full moon,' said Ratsnappy.

'And getting made up nicely,' said Sharkadder. 'With a decent mirror.'

'And sitting down in my own little hovel in front of a nice cosy fire with a hot cup of bogwater, squabbling with Hugo and listening to the rain,' said Pongwiffy.

They all looked at each other.

'Yeah!' they shouted with one accord. 'Let's go home!'

And with wild whoops, they mounted their skittish Brooms and took off into the night sky.

From the bush in the garden came the sound of straining, followed by a plop.

Mrs Molotoff had laid another egg.

A report has just come in that, somewhere high in the Misty Mountains, a gaggle of heavily bandaged Goblins are trudging home. Many miles of hardship and suffering and torment lie before them – the usual sort of stuff, but in reverse. Storm clouds are gathering, abysses are looming, packs of wolves are closing in, Abominable Snowmen lie in wait. When they get back home they won't be able to relax, for a certain Witch will come looking for them, you can bet on it.

But all this lies before them. Right now they are in good spirits. The night is balmy. The moon is full. No one has fallen down a precipice – yet. For sustenance, they have with them a rare treat – a lovely bucketful of overripe tomatoes. And, as they keep telling each other, they did it*! They have been to Gobboworld. In fact, for a few enchanted hours, they were the* heroes *of Gobboworld.*

Oh yes. They have had their moment of glory. For the moment, anyway, they are content.